THE GREAT BROWNIE TASTE-OFF

(A Yolanda's Yummery Cozy Mystery)

BOOK 1

LISA MALIGA

Book description

Cat shelter employee Yolanda Carter loves her job, but her dream is to own her own bakery. Living in Sherman Oaks, California with her tuxedo cat, her only outlet is baking treats for her friends, coworkers and family.

Her situation changes when her high school friend, Teagan Mishkin, drops by to tell her about an incredible job opportunity that will give Yolanda enough money to launch her bakery.

The job interview takes an unexpected turn and Yolanda stumbles across a scheme to close the cat shelter. She concocts a sweet plan to save the shelter and share her decadent brownies in the Great Brownie Taste-off. Assisted by her artisan parents, friends, and coworkers, will she win the taste-off and save the cats?

Includes the winning brownie recipe.

Yolanda's Yummery Cozy Mystery Series

The Great Brownie Taste-off, Book 1
The Missing Sea Captain, Book 2
A Pie to Die For, Book 3
Macarons and Murder, Book 4
To be announced, Book 5

Other Works of Fiction

Diary of a Hollywood Nobody
Hollywood After Dark: 3 Tales of Terror
I Almost Married a Narcissist
I WANT YOU: Seduction Emails from a Narcissist
Love Me, Need Me: A Narcissist's Tale
The Narcissist Chronicles: The WHOLE Story
North of Sunset
Notes from Nadir
Out of the Blue
Satan's Casting Call
September Harvest
South of Sunset
Sweet Dreams

COOKBOOKS

Baking Chocolate Cupcakes and Brownies: A Beginner's Guide
Baking French Macarons: A Beginner's Guide
Baking Macarons: The Swiss Meringue Method
Dessert Cookbook Series: A Beginner's Guide
Ruby Chocolate: A Beginner's Guide

Table of Contents

Preface

The Yolanda's Yummery series began as a fluke. It was supposed to contain a few sweet romance novels. When I wrote the second book, I thought that a cozy mystery was far more interesting to write. After that, the other books fell squarely into the sweet romance/cozy mystery genres. The problem began with the titles. Anytime the word love is seen, people assume it's a romance. The covers with their uniform pink backgrounds didn't dissuade anyone from that notion.

The series ended up consisting of four books. The least likely to be categorized as a cozy is this one, and the title remains the same: *The Great Brownie Taste-off.* Although classified as a sweet romance, for those who have read the book, the sweetness was more attributable to what Yolanda baked rather than the relationship she had with her boyfriend, Zac Field. In this version, the bond between them is a little different.

Meanwhile, I wrote more dessert cookbooks. This year, I returned to the Southern California yummery. I fixed the main problem of the magic ingredient – I removed it because it didn't seem like a necessary addition.

As for Yolanda Carter, the protagonist of this book series, she learns what happens when you imagine having your own bakery. How did she manage to get the yummery that she dreamed about for many years? Read on and find out!

Chapter 1

Yolanda Carter took a bite of the red velvet cupcake. The swirl of sweet and tangy cream cheese frosting dissolved in her mouth, followed by the rich chocolaty goodness of the cupcake. Yes, this batch was just fine, but a smattering of sprinkles would help the cupcakes stand out even more. Sprinkles were always good to have when bringing in cupcakes for Fun Food Friday. Employees and volunteers loved the tradition of sharing different types of food every week. It had been going on at the Crown Street Cat Shelter for years, and Yolanda was always happy to bring in her freshly baked cookies, cupcakes, layer cakes, or brownies.

Since it was February, but an appropriately gorgeous sunny day with temperatures promising to soar into the mid-80s, she thought that turquoise sprinkles would be a nice touch. She went over to the wooden spice rack that sat on her counter and found the sprinkles, which she gently shook on each swirled cupcake top. She loved that the rack had only decorations and her most used-and-loved vanilla and flavor extracts, rather than the twenty-four herbs and spices that had come with the housewarming present from her parents. Yolanda baked far more than she cooked; while she still had the standard spices, they were kept in the back of a cupboard at the far end of the kitchen. She'd shoved them next to some extra salt-and-pepper shaker sets she'd received as gifts years ago but hadn't used.

For a second, she admired the array of cupcakes sporting their perky blue buttons of sugar. A glance at the chalet-style cuckoo clock above the back door showed that she was running late. She swallowed the rest of the red velvet and placed the decorated cupcakes in the plastic carrier. *Shouldn't have this much sugar in the morning*, she thought, knowing she'd have to be careful about what she ate the rest of the day.

Yolanda was of average height and had an extra ten pounds on her hips that wouldn't go away, even when she went for day-long canyon hikes or rode her bike countless miles along the beachside bike trails. She had warm hazel eyes and long chestnut hair pulled back into a ponytail. She wore baggy jeans she'd bought at a resale shop, pairing them with a purple batik shirt made by her artsy mother.

Wearing comfortable clothing was necessary in her line of work.

She thought about her upcoming day. Missy Wakefield, her boss, would be there, as would Sid, the new college student, along with a couple of volunteers. Tomorrow will be another Cat Adoption Day, so there was more work than usual. She had to make sure there were plenty of adoption forms and copies of the kitten-and-cat tips booklet. Yolanda was proud of the fact that she had helped her boss write the booklet and take cute photos of some cats and kittens to enhance it. She had grown up with cats and even a few dogs, and last year had adopted Miss Chef, a classic tuxedo cat with a white stripe down her face and a perpetually curved white smile. Her dainty white paws were always kept clean, and the stripe along the front of her body was groomed several times a day. Her official name was Miss Pastry Chef, but sometimes her name was shortened to Mischief. Once, Yolanda had left a cupcake on the coffee table in the living room, as she was going to have a snack while she watched *Cupcake Battles.* The cat had jumped up and devoured the sweet treat. She learned never to leave anything edible unattended after that.

While she loved her job, especially being around a cast of approximately 175 cats and kittens 40 hours per week, she knew that earning just over minimum wage wasn't going to get her the bakery that she envisioned. Not even if she scrimped and saved every dollar she earned. Start-up fees for a tiny bakery in Los Angeles County were very high—even if she opted for a location in Whittier or somewhere less expensive than Sherman Oaks.

She picked up her pink-and-purple batik tote bag that was always filled with cat toys and packets of nutritious homemade cat treats. The four-legged residents staying at the shelter enjoyed eating her signature tuna and chicken treats.

Inside the detached garage, she unlocked her car and put the carrier in the back seat of her old silver hatchback. It was good for hauling things and occasionally visiting the gas station. It was also a source of embarrassment for her boyfriend, self-professed "ragtop-man" Zac Field.

Within a few minutes, she was approaching the small, prefabricated building with a potholed parking lot behind it. She could tell who was there by the show of vehicles: her boss's Toyota SUV, the Harley favored by part-timer Sid, Tatiana's older Jetta, and Julio's minivan. A vintage blue Schwinn bicycle with shiny chrome fenders was locked in the bike rack--Laura's ride.

On the other side of Crown Street, she noticed two men in dark shirts and slacks talking to each other. The man with a wispy fringe of blond hair was peering through a late-model camcorder as he focused on filming something behind her. The other man, with gray hair and a matching beard, was clutching a minuscule point-and-shoot digital camera. He stood on the sidewalk taking photos of what looked like the shelter or the small warehouse next to it. He happened to notice her and quickly turned, heading farther down the block.

As she reached into her car to grab her stuff, she saw them scurry over to a burgundy Lexus sedan and get inside. It took off in the opposite direction and turned down Warren Street, disappearing from view. *That's odd*, she thought.

She balanced her tote bag in one hand and the carrier in the other and opened the back door of the cat shelter. The smell hit the instant she stepped inside, the ripe stench of dozens of cats. She couldn't wear her favorite perfume, as some of the cats were allergic to harsh aromas, even though it smelled like freshly baked cookies. So, she had to close her nose and concentrate on her adored little charges. The meow-chorus greeted her, as a group of cats made it evident that they knew she had special treats for them. Even as she walked up to the back entrance, she could hear the kitty cat glee club as her diehard fans called out.

Resembling the Pied Piper of cats, Yolanda rushed to the closed door with the NO CATS/EMPLOYEES ONLY sign prominently displayed. On cue, it opened for her. She gratefully stepped inside, as the size-twelve track shoe of Sid gently nudged the large calico leader aside.

"So sorry I'm late," she said, the door slamming behind her. In the hallway, the meowers doubled their efforts, underscoring the ruckus with their frantic claws scratching the door.

Gangly young Sid, who wore his usual faded black jeans and T-shirt, looked in the direction of the noise and laughed. "Reminds me of zombies," he said.

"I know what you mean!" She placed the carrier on the scratched former dining room table in the center of the room. In the shelter, the break room also served as a conference room. She plunked her tote bag next to it. The room, walled in cinder blocks and painted in gaudy neon like a sunset on steroids, always made her eyes hurt for a few seconds. "I have red velvet cupcakes."

Missy walked in and kept the strident cats at bay with her fast entrance. The older woman had hip-length black hair with graying roots. Baggy cargo pants sported bulges of telltale cat treats in the multitude of pockets, and a bulky navy sweatshirt attempted to hide her girth. "Hey, Yolanda," she said, observing the younger woman removing the lid from the carrier. "You brought my favorite cupcakes!"

"You always say that, Missy."

"It's always true. Good news! This time, we have plates and napkins." Missy went over to the small table that held a coffee maker with a fresh pot that was almost full. "Discount store sale so we got the pretty ones!"

Yolanda walked over to the table and saw a stack of pink-patterned cupcake-motif plates and matching napkins.

Sid ambled over, poured himself a cup of coffee, and plated a cupcake. In one bite, he managed to remove all the frosting. A second large bite, and the cupcake was gone. "I'm a frosting-first kinda guy."

Yolanda laughed. "Just like my dad!" She touched her nose, seeing a smudge of frosting on the tip of his nose.

Sid smiled and wiped it away. "I love any cupcake with cream cheese frosting. Or chocolate. But yours are always the best."

She beamed. "Thanks, Sid."

Another clamor from the cats as they tried to catch their attention when the door opened a crack. A flash of wavy golden-brown hair and the angular face of the morning volunteer, Laura, was seen when she peeked in and waved.

"Missy, you have a call on line two."

"Hey Laura, have a cupcake," Yolanda said.

"Are they gluten-free?"

"Sorry, no," Yolanda replied.

"Bummer," Laura said as she closed the door. There was a yelp from a cat that almost got its tail caught in the door.

Yolanda took a red velvet for herself, foregoing the coffee in favor of a bottle of water from the fridge. *This'll be my last cupcake today*, she thought. Opening the bottle and taking a sip, she closed it and quickly finished her snack. The remaining cupcakes tempted her to stay longer and indulge her sugar craving. Her next job was anything but sweet. She mentally braced herself for the dreaded duty of litter box cleanup. Stashing her tote bag in her locker, she removed a packet of the tuna treats and put them in her back pocket. Then it was time to face the feline hordes in the sunroom, where they roamed free.

She tentatively pulled the door open a crack to see if there were any nearby. Fortunately, there weren't any, so she was able to leave the break room without having to fend any off. Sometimes she had to resort to throwing spare treats in the hallway about ten yards to the right so she could leave unscathed and not have to chase any strays around the room.

The large sunroom was where dozens of cats spent time together on a daily basis. All sorts of carpeted climbing and sleeping towers kept them off the floor. Secondhand couches and chairs served as beds, as did the cushions. The wooden floor was also home to lounging cats. Small groups of them occupied a few carpets and rugs. Three strategically placed litter boxes were in dire need of waste disposal. Yolanda stopped off at the supply closet to don a pair of latex gloves, grab a clean plastic scoop, and take a wheeled garbage can with her. Just as she approached the first litter box, a young tabby leapt out of it, leaving behind an uncovered mess. Worse than that was the diarrhea deposited about a yard away from the box. Sid walked in carrying a young tiger cat and noticed the situation. "I guess Doc couldn't make it to the box in time."

Yolanda shook her head. "At least two or three times a day he goes there. Someone was being sarcastic when they named him Doc."

"Diarrhea Doc," Sid said.

After she finished cleaning out the plastic boxes and refilling them with generic-brand cat litter, she sprinkled a layer of baking soda on top of the clean clay surface. That gesture wasn't appreciated as she was almost shoved aside by a couple of eager cats. Returning her cleaning supplies, she walked down the hallway and saw Laura putting a large calico cat into its cage. "This is the sixth time Cameo's been passed over for adoption," she said.

Petting the cat, Yolanda saw the animal's downcast expression. She reached into her back pocket and pulled out two squares of the treat. Cameo enthusiastically ate them and purred. "Don't worry, Cameo, you'll find a good home."

Looking at the other cages, she made sure all the occupants got a couple of tuna bits. Cage number 23 was now home to a muscular shorthaired black cat with a single white whisker amid his black whiskers. Upon seeing Yolanda, he rubbed up against the bars. She handed him a few of the treats and he gobbled them down loudly. He stuck his paw between the bars, and she stroked it. "When did he get here?"

"Mr. Whisker got here this morning. He was sitting on the back doorstep looking like he was waiting to be let inside."

"Another drop-off," Yolanda said. "Seems like it's every day now."

Laura nodded. "You're right. It does."

Yolanda sighed and handed out treats to every cat behind bars. She felt like they were little prisoners in the cages. They always had enough food and water. They were taken out for exercise, but all needed a real home, what most people involved with the shelter called a forever home.

Missy stopped by as Laura returned to the reception desk at the main entrance. "I think you should be selling those cat treats."

"Well, uh, I don't add preservatives and I don't have a commercial kitchen. I just like to bake cat treats on the side."

While she enjoyed making the feline delicacies, they weren't nearly as fun and exciting as coming up with a new cookie or cupcake recipe. It wasn't like determining if a chocolate caramel pecan cookie needed to be crisp or soft. Or what colors to make her favorite buttercream frosting. As she was walking down the hall to fill the food bowls, a Siamese mix ran out of the reception area followed closely by Julio.

With his marathoner's training, it didn't take the man long to nab the errant cat and return it to the smaller room.

"Hey, Julio, you were here early this morning, right?"

The older man chuckled. "You know me, I love to get up early."

"Did you see anything weird this morning? Like two guys with cameras and video equipment taking pictures?"

"People make movies everywhere."

"But of a cat shelter?"

He shrugged. "Why not? Location scouts, maybe? And if they made a movie here, we'd place a lot of cats in forever homes."

Yolanda smiled. "Wow, that'd be great. I just got suspicious. They had a real fancy new car."

"Even more likely they're making a movie."

She looked at her watch and saw it was time to report for front office duty and deal with Ozzie the office manager. Inside the cramped office, she went to the scratched-up desk where the elderly computer sat, decorated with colorful sticky notes along the monitor's edges. The wallpaper showed a fluffy Persian cat. The chair's added cushion held a huge tabby that was curled up, snoring and purring. Ozzie weighed nearly thirty pounds and his general duties consisted of eating, sleeping, shuffling over to his private litter box in the corner, and returning to slumberland in his favorite chair. Working with Ozzie meant that he had to sit in the employee's lap while they used the computer. Yolanda helped compose the email newsletter and add more names to the contact list. Ozzie noticed her, sniffed her hand, and returned to his extended sleeping schedule.

Finally, quitting time rolled around. She would have to work on Saturday but had Sunday off.

Only Missy was still inside doing the paperwork. Yolanda put her empty cupcake carrier in her car and did a perimeter check to make certain there were no drop-offs and no escapees. Nothing. The last place she looked at was the dumpster on the east side of the building and it was a case of saving the worst for last. The stench wasn't for the faint-hearted, and discovering abandoned felines was something Yolanda and her co-workers dreaded finding.

Picking up the stick that was kept next to the big garbage bin, she opened the lid, bracing herself for a nasal assault. It was bad, and she concentrated on looking for any movement from a bag or wads of towels or rags; gently poking the long stick around, finding and hearing nothing. Relieved, she was about to shut the lid when a loud shout of "incoming!" made her look up.

A dark object was flying in her direction. Behind that she saw a flash of light from a pair of eyeglasses catching the last rays of the setting sun. A man on a bicycle sped westward on Crown Street, concealed by the shadowy buildings.

The object was a backpack that fell next to the dumpster. Letting the lid fall with a crash, she bent down to retrieve it. *Oh no, I hope there's no one in here,* she thought. But the weight of the bag wasn't heavy, and she unlatched it, finding a crumpled piece of paper in the main compartment. "I should tell Missy about this," she said to herself, knowing that no one was around.

Rushing back inside, she found her boss putting on her jacket. "Hey Missy, some guy on a bike just dropped this off."

Her boss frowned, "What's in it?"

Yolanda put the bag on her boss's desk. "I just checked the main area, not the pockets."

"Okay," Missy said, rummaging through the navy knapsack with a broken strap. "Glad there's no cats in here."

She pulled out the paper. "Notebook paper," she said, uncrumpling it. "It says 'get out of here' in all caps."

"Get out of the shelter? The block? The city?"

Missy shrugged. "I know less than you. Did you see what the man looked like?"

"No, I was doing the dumpster check and had the lid up. The knapsack fell on the ground, so that's why I'm super glad there wasn't a cat in it. I only know it was a man on a bike wearing glasses. It happened so fast, you know."

"He threw it at you?"

"Yeah. And he shouted incoming."

"Incoming? That's all he said?"

"Yeah. And he rode off—fast."

"Look, it's Friday night, it's Van Nuys, and people are weird. Just put it back where it belongs and forget about it," said her boss.

"Okay," she said, going back to the dumpster and tossing it inside. Yolanda hurried to her car, mulling over the strangeness of the incident.

Chapter 2

Miss Chef jumped on Yolanda's bed just after nine o'clock and began purring. Grumbling, she sat up and the cat meowed and rubbed against her.

"Okay, I'm awake." She pushed the bedding aside and swung her legs over the bedside. Standing up, she plunged her feet into her slippers and shuffled toward the bedroom door.

Almost hugging her ankles as she walked down the carpeted hallway, Miss Chef jumped over her feet as they entered the kitchen. The cat ran towards the empty cobalt glass food bowl handcrafted by Yolanda's father, Frederick Carter. It was a one-of-a-kind hand-blown glass creation. The disappointed cat looked at the empty dish, not caring that it was created just for her; it was empty and that caused her to meow loudly and repeatedly.

"I'm getting your breakfast," Yolanda said as she went to the cabinet and opened it. Pulling out a bag of healthy organic chicken and dried liver bits, she poured a handful into the bowl. She knew her cat was hungry by the way she gobbled it down and soon there was a look that said *I want seconds.* "Later, Miss Chef," Yolanda said to the cat who cleaned her paws as though that display might elicit more food.

The sun was shining in her favorite room of the house highlighting the stainless steel appliances. A butcher block topped island held her precious chrome KitchenAid stand mixer. Two of the wooden sides of the island held much of her baking ware, and the other two had shelves filled with her cookbook collection.

Since it was Sunday, why not give Miss Chef a special treat? She opened a drawer where she had samples of cat food and found a packet of chicken bone broth which was slurped with gusto.

She made her cream of wheat topped with pure Vermont maple syrup. Sitting at the kitchen table, she read an old cookie recipe book and decided to make the Brazilian coffee cookies. Adding more cinnamon and a dash of nutmeg would make them even warmer. "I'll need to change the white flour to rice flour." That would alter them to gluten free cookies for her mother who swore off most "glutenish products" and kept her size four figure. That's why they were often mistaken for sisters plus the fact that

Abby Carter taught Pilates as well as made batik and tie-dye bags and clothing. Thanks to her, Yolanda had a collection of customized batik-print aprons in all her favorite colors.

While the cookies were baking, she checked her voicemail. She pulled her cell phone and iPad from a kitchen drawer and set them down on the counter. She heard one from Zac Field, her boyfriend of eight months. He must have known she would be home baking and on cue the cuckoo clock chirped twelve times.

She was unable to hear the rest of the hourly cuckoo show because it was drowned out by the deafening twin turbo engine in the driveway.

Yolanda didn't need to glance out the window to hear the BMW M3 convertible's engine being revved in front of her garage. The noise abated and his engine was switched off, filling the area with silence. When he appeared, she saw him close the door with his hip to avoid touching the gleaming surface. The jet-black car was almost a decade-old, but it had been ceramic coated, so it looked brand new. He wore his white golf shirt with the Green Palms Mini Golf Course logo on his chest. On the back it read GOLF PRO. He wore a golf cap and khakis. As he strode toward the door, he slid his sunglasses onto his hat.

She opened the door for him, and he smiled and kissed her quickly. He sniffed the air. "Hey, Yolanda; whatcha been baking?"

Yolanda glanced at the clock above them and rushed back to the oven, switching on the light, and looking through the glass window at the baking cookies. She put on her oven mitts, opened the door, and felt the rush of heat and smelled the perky aroma of coffee-flavored cookies. The two dozen cookies were at that golden stage, and she removed the sheet and placed it on top of a waiting towel. She sniffed them once more, shut the oven door with her foot, and took a thin pancake turner and moved them to a wire rack. Zac stood nearby and watched. After the last cookie was transferred, he reached over to grab one, but she gently slapped his hand.

"They need to cool for about five minutes before you can..."

He picked up a soft cookie and put it in his mouth, cringing. "This is hot."

"That's why I said you need to wait."

"But it's good. What kind is it?"

"These are Brazilian coffee cookies."

"Nice." He was about to reach for another one, but she moved the rack. "So, you think about working at a bakery?"

"Nope. You know I want to own my own bakery. But I've decided not to call it a bakery--it'll be known as Yolanda's Yummery."

He shook his head. "Huh? Yolanda's whatery?"

"Yolanda's Yummery. Because I'm going to bake everything there myself and everything will be yummy. Cookies, cakes, cupcakes, and brownies to start with."

"I've never heard of a yummery before." He noticed her iPad sitting on the counter and picked it up. "Let me see about a yummery in..." He typed in the word and waited. Scrolling down the screen with his eyes following his fingers. "Nothing. No yummery. Yum. Yummy...but not yummery. People won't know what it is. They'll walk in and go 'Are we supposed to say yum?'"

She giggled as she went over to him, and he handed her the tablet. "See? Nothing listed."

"That's good. I'll be creating my own brand."

"If you want to bake so badly, why don't you work at Costco or Ralphs? They have good bakeries."

"Have you tasted their cookies? They use margarine or canola oil. That's the worst oil to use as the refined version is...well don't get me started on that. Of course, they add preservatives. The cookies are still good past their expiration date. "

"What's wrong with that?"

"Cookies shouldn't last that long. You wouldn't drink sour milk, would you?"

"Yolanda, starting your own business takes lots of money and time. There's no job security or benefits. Most businesses fail within the first year. Work at a big bakery and you get salary and benefits. I know Jay who manages the Ralphs over on Woodman because he takes his sons golfing at Green Palms. I can put in a good word for you, and you can get hired."

"Wow, thanks for the support, Zac." She felt a shiver race down her spine at the suggestion. "You know how creative I am and how I care about the quality of everything I bake. I care about every ingredient that goes into my desserts." She reached over, took a cookie off the rack, and bit into it. "This is how I want to serve them to people--warm and freshly made."

"They won't stay that way." He reached for another one and she gently pushed his hand away.

"I'll sell them as fast as I make them. And these are for my parents. My mom wants to stay away from wheat and dairy products."

"That sucks. I like my pizza to have extra cheese."

She chuckled. "Yeah. So do I."

"I'm working till seven, so if you want to meet me at the Burbank AMC we can see a movie tonight."

"Okay, sounds good. I'll text you when I leave my parents' place, but I should be able to make it by then."

He glanced at the clock above the door, kissed her, and left. She watched as he got into his car and an instant later the engine rumbled to life and was gunned twice. The car raced down the short driveway and onto the street. Yolanda cringed at the thought of someone on the sidewalk or a hapless bicyclist in the area, as they would've been flattened by his careless driving. Fortunately, she didn't hear any discordant noises. Miss Chef was in the living room, so the cat was safe.

She pulled out another handcrafted piece of glasswork by her dad: a blue-and-yellow-striped cookie jar and saw there were only a few double chocolate chip cookies left. Adding three of the coffee cookies, she put the rest of them in a new plastic container that she would give to her parents. The phone rang and she answered it, surprised to see Teagan Mishkin's name on the screen. She answered after the second ring.

"Hey, Teagan; how's it going?"

"Yo, I'm doing great! You home?"

"I'm here, but I'm going to visit my parents soon."

"That's okay, I just wanted to tell you about my new job and thought you might be interested in earning $900 a night."

"Nine hundred a night? Is it legal?"

"Of course it's legal. I'll tell you about it in person. I'll be there around one or one-thirty."

"Sure, okay," Yolanda tentatively said as the phone went dead. She set it on the counter and walked back into her bedroom. Miss Chef approached from behind and rushed into her room, jumping onto the bed. Yolanda sat down next to the cat and stroked her back. "I wonder what kind of job pays that much money? Something in sales? Something tells me it's not in a bakery." The cat rubbed against her knee. "Well, time to clean up and get dressed and hear what mischief Teagan's up to!" She kissed the cat on top of her head.

She went over to her closet, pulled open the accordion door and after flipping hangers past her, settled on a purple batik blouse that was given to her by her mother last Christmas. The lavender Capri pants came from a discount store, and she opted for black ballet flats. After showering and getting dressed, she returned to the kitchen to wait for her friend.

A shiny red Mercedes convertible drove up to the garage door, almost hitting it. In the early afternoon sunlight, the new car sparkled and shone like a precious ruby. Yolanda opened her door and stepped outside to see the vehicle. Who was driving such a luxurious sports car? The car door opened and a model thin young woman with a mass of bleached-blonde curls piled on top of her head stepped out. A black minidress clung to her frame, leaving little to the imagination. She wore designer heels covered with rhinestones and carried a matching handbag that twinkled as ostentatiously as her car and shoes. "Hey girlfriend!" Teagan waved her hand and the obvious orange talons had tiny rhinestones affixed to the tips.

Teagan scurried across the concrete driveway, her heels clicking with each step. "You like my new car? It's safe here, right? I don't have to lock it, do I?"

"No, Teagan, you know this is a very quiet and safe neighborhood."

"Great. It looks nice." Teagan looked across the street and to the left.

"There's a good neighborhood watch program and …"

She stopped scrutinizing the neighborhood and looked back at Yolanda. "Listen, I have some awesome news for you." She began jumping from one sparkly stiletto to the other.

"Come on in, Teagan," she said, gesturing for her friend to follow her into the kitchen. "I have some Brazilian coffee cookies and I made some iced tea."

Teagan patted her flat stomach, sucking it in even more to emphasize the washboard abdominal muscles. "I have to watch my weight, but thanks."

"You're really skinny," she said to the girl she'd known since they'd sat next to each other in tenth-grade English class.

"Well, I'm rich now! And you can be too. I know you don't want to work at that cat place and want to have your own bakery. If you work where I do you can earn as much as me--maybe even more!"

"How do you earn $900 a night? I'm almost afraid to ask…"

"I'm just a cocktail waitress. As long as I show some cleavage and smile a lot, I get tips. Of course, I have to serve the drinks, not spill 'em and not mix up the orders. I gotta work really fast and wear a sexy outfit like this." She did a spin, holding up her hands and giggling. "Oh, and sometimes I dance. I don't have any downtime at work, and the clientele are men--professional men. Working men, but some of them are super loaded. Really rich men. The best of all the men are the rich men that are really hot."

"Where is this place?" Yolanda was warming up to the concept of earning three figures a night, even if she would have to wear a mini skirt and hustle drinks.

"Near the edge of Beverly Hills in West L.A." She pulled out her iPhone housed in a bedazzling magenta case and pressed a button. A single push of a button meant that person was highly ranked in Teagan's world. And it was a two-sided deal as the phone call was answered within seconds. "Rocky, I have my friend Yolanda Carter here and if you can…what?" She paused. "Yeah. I know. I've known her since high school. She's the same age as me." She nodded, looking down at the floor. "Right, I'll tell her." She disconnected and put her phone back into her bag. "Rocky says he can see you any time before five."

"What do I wear for the interview?"

"You're fine. You don't even need to bring a resume. Just go to 11236 Marina del Mar Street. It's still not listed on the internet but it's near the 405. If you don't find any street parking, there's a valet out back. Tell him you're there for an interview and you can park for free."

Yolanda keyed in the address on her iPad. She looked at her friend and smiled. "I want my bakery and if this will get it…"

An hour later, Yolanda was circling the block looking for a parking space, finding one in front of a martial arts school next door to the Wicked Fun Gentlemen's Club. When she got out of the car, she saw the meter still had forty minutes on it, but the sight of the word "wicked" and the term "gentlemen's club" made her pause. It was a two-story building. Nothing unusual looking about it except for the name.

Reluctantly she headed up the sidewalk and into the building. Inside she walked down a long and dark hallway. To her left she heard the muffled sound of heavy bass. At the end of the hall was a box office like in a movie theatre. Prominently displayed were NO SMOKING and MUST BE OVER 21 signs. A cashier wearing oblong red glasses pointed to the sign that showed the prices. "I know you're a chick but admission's still not free."

"I'm here to see Rocky about a job," she explained to the cashier who was reading a current issue of *Cosmopolitan* magazine. The cashier nodded, picked up the phone, and hit a speed dial number. "What's your name?" she asked.

"My name's Yolanda."

"Good name. Rocky, a Yolanda's here to see you."

The cashier pushed her eyeglasses up the bridge of her narrow nose and resumed reading the magazine. "He'll be right down."

"Um, thanks," Yolanda said as she moved to the entrance between the hallway and the club. The music was a little louder.

A short dark-haired man opened the door and stepped into the hallway, as the door slammed shut behind him. He gave her a smile as he appraised Yolanda, from her natural brunette hair pulled into a ponytail down to her black flats. In between his scouting expedition, he'd lingered on her salable assets noting her average cleavage and the hips she was self-conscious about. His narrow eyes brightened, and his flushed round face grew redder beneath the overhead chandelier.

"You're Yolanda … Teagan's friend?" he asked, reaching out to shake her hand, the blue sharkskin jacket's sleeve showing too much patterned cuff. He pronounced it as TEE-gan when it was always pronounced TAY-gan. She nodded and shook his hand, feeling the sweaty heat as she longed to wipe her hand on her pants, but he was intently observing her, so she did nothing other than stand there at the edge of the Wicked Fun Gentlemen's Club.

"Teagan's really good," Rocky said, as he continued staring at Yolanda. "Follow me," he said, opening the door for her, and watched as she walked into the club. He chuckled. "Teagan will do anything to keep our customers very happy. She keeps them happy; she keeps the employees happy and most of all she keeps me happy." He winked and licked his wet lips. "You and Teagan are good friends?"

"Um yeah, we've known each other since our sophomore year of high school, so about ten years." She looked around at the club. It wasn't as tacky as she'd initially thought when she first drove up and saw the place. There were many tiny round tables with black tablecloths, plush looking burgundy booths along the outer walls, and a soft, gray-carpeted floor. Plenty of spotlights shone above the horseshoe shaped stage. Techno music pulsated and her ears began aching at the noise level. Did she really want to work in a place like this? A few men and couples gawked at the onstage entertainment. Wrapping herself around the pole was a petite woman with long hair that touched the stage floor. She arched her back and scissored her legs in various positions. All she wore was a tiny, spangled bikini bottom and an equally skimpy top.

Yolanda spotted a scowling bouncer with an ear mic. "Come Yolanda," Rocky said. "I audition you now." He hurried over to a door beneath a stairwell. "Here, I get you a costume." He opened the door and reached into a closet, pulling out something black and shiny. "Here it is." He extended a tiny piece of spangled fabric, and she accepted it. "Now, you go to the dressing room and put it on and meet me at the stage. Go upstairs, last door on the left."

He scurried away before she had a chance to say anything. She looked at the flimsy bikini bottom and wondered if it would fit her. There was no bikini top. She went upstairs and walked down a burgundy-carpeted hallway with closed doors on both sides. All were numbered like in a hotel. Passing the first door, she overheard loud thumping disco music, but it didn't mask the sounds of shouts and moans. She scurried along, not wanting to hear anything else. "Think about the yummery," she said softly. "Think about being my own boss and baking..."

Outside the last closed door, she knocked hesitantly. Was she supposed to go in there? No music emanated from the room. As she put her hand on the doorknob, the door suddenly opened, and a tall woman in a snug sundress stood there. "Yes?"

"Um, hey, my name's Yolanda. Rocky told me to change into this..." She held out the tiny bit of fabric and the woman laughed.

"Hey, I'm Cherie and I don't think that would fit you. I don't think that would fit my four-year-old." She held it up and pulled at the flimsy bottom, which broke. "There, now you don't have to wear it." She tossed it back to Yolanda and slammed the door, her laughter even louder than before.

"Wow, she's a jerk." Yolanda said quietly to herself. She stood there for a few seconds before turning around and hurrying down the hallway. She headed downstairs to the stage. She held the bikini in one hand; her purse in the other and she thought she'd leave the costume with the cashier and go to her parents' house. But Rocky strode over to her. "Where is your costume?"

She held out the torn bikini bottom. "Um, it broke before I could even try it on."

Rocky sighed and glanced at his flashy gold watch. "Okay, okay, you go up there and dance and take off your clothes. That's good."

Yolanda paused, looking at the owner, the realization of what the place was and what she was expected to do made all too clear. Dance and take off her clothes? Even her boyfriend hadn't seen her without them. The least she'd worn was a modest one-piece swimsuit the last time they went to the beach. And she'd worn a towel over her hips until she reached the edge of the ocean.

Nine hundred dollars a night, Yolanda. Was it possible to earn that much money? She gave a flicker of a smile. This wasn't a forever job. It wasn't a long-term job. It was a temporary job that would have huge benefits. Approaching the stage, she was puzzled as to how she'd get up there until she saw a small staircase at the side. Tentatively, she walked up the steps and stood near the side of the stage. Rocky positioned himself near the sunglass-wearing DJ. "Give it up for Yolanda who's auditioning as one of the Wicked Fun Wanton Women! She'll be dancing to a 1970s classic, 'I Will Survive.'"

The song began playing and she saw some customers, mostly men, move over to the stage and nearby bar area. All attention was focused on her as she stood there blindly staring straight ahead, the overhead lights too bright.

"Move those hips!" shouted a bearded man.

"Take off your shirt!" This from the woman who had moved aside, giving Yolanda the spotlight.

Rocky lifted his arms and waved them. "Use the pole!"

Startled, she looked at her potential boss, then at the shiny chrome pole that she almost walked into. What the previous "wanton woman" had been doing on it in her minimal attire wasn't something that she really wanted to contemplate. All she'd seen was what the acrobatic woman had been up to, and her own skills in that area were nonexistent. She had some upper body strength due to lifting lots of cats in and out of cages and carrying food and litterbags around the shelter. Baking wasn't for the weak, either, as it entailed lots of stirring, pouring, lifting and moving--often very rapidly to avoid anything being burned in the oven. It also required quick thinking and decent math skills.

As Gloria Gaynor sang the theme song for two generations of women who'd endured heartbreak, Yolanda Carter was trying to figure out how to navigate a 12-foot pole. Maybe if she grabbed it and swung around it like a playground ride in a park that would suffice. She had to take off her clothing and pilot herself around a slender immovable object and it seemed like a loser take the prize situation. The music played as she contemplated her next move. Projecting her personality to the audience: zero percent. Likelihood of obtaining the job: also, zero percent.

The real exotic dancer returned, followed by the haughty Cherie who shoved her aside and began climbing up the pole; she flashed her shimmering silver bikini.

Rocky walked over to the steps and signaled to Yolanda. "I don't think this is the job for you." He shook his head. "My mother was beautiful when she was young, but she couldn't do it. My wife is very beautiful, but no, she couldn't do it. You see, men don't want you to be shy. They want you to be sexy like your friend Teagan, and just dance and show off your beautiful body. And she must be an excellent cocktail waitress also."

Yolanda stepped down to ground level and still was taller than Rocky. "You're right. I've done office work and…"

"You type letters like a secretary?" he asked.

"Yes, of course I can type."

"Good, I can pay you really good. I will give you a typing test and if you type a lotta words you get the job. No taking off your clothes." He turned and headed for the back of the club.

She followed him through the club and past a svelte woman sporting a red bikini. Her pale skin was enhanced with glitter dust, and it was also sprayed in her wavy hair. Another woman walked closely behind and sneered at Yolanda.

They entered his large office. On a corner of the table sat a new laptop. A sectional tan leather couch ran along one side of the office. Yolanda thought that he'd have to pay way more than what she earned at the shelter to get her interested in his place. She knew the salary wouldn't come close to $900 per night but the thought of leaving her clothing on was appealing.

"Now if this doesn't work, we got a kitchen. We make good bar food … burgers, fries, chicken strips, and chicken wings. Sometimes one of the cooks don't show up. Can you cook?"

Totally taken aback, Yolanda just nodded.

"But first let's see about the secretary, no, administrative assistant job."

He leaned over his desk and grabbed a piece of paper, handing it to her. She saw that it was a letter; he told her to type it and that he'd be back in two minutes. He glanced at his watch and walked out. She sat down and saw an icon-covered main screen. Hurriedly, she found the word processing program, clicked it open, and began typing the contents of the letter.

Mr. Rocky Montoya

Wicked Fun Gentlemen's Club

11236 Marina Del Mar Street

Los Angeles, CA 90064

Dear Mr. Montoya:

Subject: Acquiring the Crown Street Cat Shelter--12049 S. Crown Street, Van Nuys, CA 91401

We have thoroughly explored the options of leasing this property and/or other nearby properties for the purpose of acquiring the building now housing the Crown Street Cat Shelter.

As agents of the corporation known as Freeze N Bake Corporation, Inc. [formerly Montoya Enterprises], headquartered in Altadena, California, we have chosen the site at 12049 S. Crown Street, as it meets all our agents' needs to have a facility that can adequately house the storage required for a regional warehousing unit for the Freeze N Bake Corporation.

It would be necessary to have the current residents, both humans and felines, to be moved out no later than July 31 of this year. Our interest is in being able to adequately and completely reconstruct the premises so that they may conform to our usual high quality and hard-line controlled facilities in which to store our fine fresh frozen products. We consider it of utmost importance that we will be fully functional by November 1 of this year at the Crown Street location.

We have outlined the terms in our enclosed contract, which you may have your lawyer scrutinize.

We expect to hear from you shortly.

Sincerely yours,

W. E. Thurston, Esq.

Just as she typed the period, Rocky returned. She looked at him but didn't see him. The cat shelter was being bought out and shut down? Where would the cats go? Where would her coworkers go? Did they even know about it? Did Missy know about it? If she did, why didn't she mention anything? After all, Missy had been there the longest.

"So, you just print out the document and I look at it," Rocky said.

She nodded, hitting the print button and seeing the paper shoot out of a printer behind his desk. He sat down and looked at it. "My secretary left me on Friday. I need to..." The phone on his desk rang and he paused, realizing it wasn't in front of him but buried beneath the contents strewn across the glass surface. He knocked over a sheaf of papers and found his cell phone. He flipped it open, looking at the screen. "What is it?"

There was a pause, and she overheard a high-pitched voice of either a woman or a child. Yolanda looked around the room and then down at her lap. The contents she'd just typed were numbing in their portent.

"Yes, right. I be right there." He clicked his phone shut and shoved it into his suit coat pocket. "I have to go. My wife needs … maybe you come back here tomorrow? We can continue our interview then." He glanced at his watch. "Yes, come here Monday at six and we'll talk more. It'll be a second interview. I offer a great competitive salary and maybe some benefits. If you agree with terms, you can start then."

She got up, too surprised to do anything other than nod her head. She followed him out the door of his office, which he shut behind him, checking the lock. A brassy blonde-haired woman with a bob rushed up the stairs, holding a garment bag. "Hey Rocky I'm gonna kill it tonight--got a posse of homies comin'--in more ways than one!"

Yolanda stopped and stared at her for an instant and quickly walked downstairs. She was still reeling with the news of the shelter's impending closure. Was it legal? Could she contact the media about it? A strip club associated with a place that made crappy stuff that you microwaved into dessert and thought you were baking? She stumbled over to her car, not seeing the new red Mercedes shooting out of the parking lot. It was the same make and model that Teagan drove.

Chapter 3

Yolanda took the usual series of freeways that led to her parents' house in Laguna Beach. She rolled the window down and enjoyed the ocean breeze blowing into the car. Usually, being near the ocean helped her troubles disappear and her mind and body relax. But not today, not with what she'd witnessed on a computer inside that strip joint office. How could she tell her parents that she'd even considered working in such a place?

She drove up Sunny Glen Drive to the white two-story, red Spanish-stucco-roofed house on a hilltop overlooking the ocean. Yolanda smiled when she saw it and parked on one side of the curved driveway. The cookie tin with the Santa Claus motif sat on the floor in the back of the car covered with a striped kitchen towel. She retrieved the tin, shut the car door, and hurried up to the driveway and over to the front door.

Whenever her parents were expecting her, they left the door unlocked. She stepped inside the large foyer, the expanse of patterned Terrazzo floor sparkling in the late afternoon sunshine. The abundance of windows let in the sunlight.

At the base of the dramatic curved stairway, she looked up and saw her mother heading down it, lightly touching the banister. Her long curly hair only had a few silvery streaks contrasting with the natural auburn color. She wore a turquoise and white shorts outfit that showed off her slender figure. Abby Carter was in great shape as she was a part-time Pilates instructor. Rushing downstairs, she greeted her daughter with a hug.

"Hi sweetheart. Glad you could make it."

Yolanda smiled and returned the hug. "Hi Mom, missed you but..."

She slipped off her shoes and her bare feet touched the stone floor of the hallway.

"No buts, you're here now," Abby said as she made a right turn. Yolanda followed her mother. She envied her parents' spacious French country kitchen with all the cookery amenities such as a double-door fridge tucked behind sage green cabinetry. The centerpiece was the six-burner range and new stainless steel double ovens. The green and black island housed the dishwasher, a warming drawer, and other cabinets. Just like Yolanda's kitchen island, both end shelves were stuffed with cookbooks.

Along the corner sat the U-shaped breakfast nook. Plush green-and-yellow plaid seats contrasted with the large, reclaimed cherry wood table. The French doors revealed a spectacular sea view. Sunset was in a couple of hours and the blue sky was already showing hints of orange that would be the main color along the coastline. Yolanda always loved the warm sunset glow.

Abby set the cookie container on the table and opened it. "Oh, my, I can smell the coffee and the butter."

"Brazilian coffee cookies, Mom."

"They smell delicious, as usual." Abby said as she bent over to fully appreciate the aroma.

"Do I hear my favorite daughter?" In strode a stocky blond man wearing a red and navy batik shirt and baggy tan shorts. Frederick Carter's blue eyes brightened upon seeing Yolanda and he embraced her in a bear hug. "Always glad to see the best baker in America." He smiled and spotted the new addition on the table. They pulled away and went to sit down, both looking at the open cookie tin.

Abby hurried over to the cabinet next to the sink where she pulled three small red porcelain plates from the shelf above her. "Let's only have one each so we don't ruin our appetite."

"What's for dinner, Mom?"

"Vegetarian burritos with my special corn salsa and baked blue corn tostada chips and…"

"And a pot roast!" Frederick winked.

"Very funny, dear. What kind of tea do you want, honey?"

"Whatever you're having, honey," replied Frederick.

"I'm asking our daughter."

"What Dad said."

A few minutes later, Abby placed three mugs bearing the colorful Abby's Batik Creations logo on a tray along with the plates. She set the tray on the table and soon they all had their mugs in front of them, and cookies on the plates. Abby was the first to bite into the hours-old cookie and slowly chewed a tiny piece, closing her eyes as she did so. "Dear, this is so flavorful."

Frederick bit into half of his and nodded. "Our girl can bake, no question." He finished his cookie and looked at the container, reaching for it. "That was kind of on the small side, so I need another one."

Abby giggled as she pulled the tin away from him. "Oh, no you don't, Frederick."

Yolanda snapped hers in half and then in half again. "Glad you like 'em so much!" She ate a quarter of it and sighed. "I wish I could bake full time in my own yummery. And I'm so worried about the shelter."

"What does that have to do with baking, dear?" her mother asked.

Yolanda glanced at the ocean and then back at her parents who sat across from her. Even though they had been married for twenty-nine years, they still sat close together.

"Well, I just found out that some company wants to shut the shelter down this summer."

"What are you saying, dear? What company?"

"Freeze N Bake."

Frederick took a sip of tea and set his mug down. "Freeze N Bake? Isn't that the frozen cookie dough that you buy in the supermarket and microwave it, so it looks like a real cookie but tastes like crap?"

"Who microwaves cookies?" Abby asked.

"You'd be surprised, dear."

"I'm puzzled--why would they want to buy a cat shelter?"

"Probably the cost. It's in the Valley in an industrial area." He had a swig of tea. "How did you find this out? From your boss?"

Yolanda shook her head. How was she going to tell her parents that she'd been applying for a job in a strip club? Well, that she was too shy for that, but she'd still been considering working in the office of one. They knew Teagan was far more adventurous than she was, so it wouldn't be a huge surprise when she told them of her high school friend's current occupation. Her parents listened as she revealed her recent adventure in the Wicked Fun Gentlemen's Club. Afterwards, Frederick put his arm around his wife and daughter. "The way I see it you have two choices, Yolanda."

Using her name meant he was being serious. She looked at his face with the blondish-gray beard.

Carson rushed into the room chasing a bug. The tabby leapt up onto Abby's lap and began purring.

"See, this is a conundrum. You wouldn't be happy working there even if it pays double what you're getting at the shelter. Maybe no *scheiss* to clean up but the types of situations you'd be seeing isn't for the likes of you. But if you can get a copy of that letter you can go to the press and make a huge stink about it. You say they need to be out this summer?"

"Yeah, July 31. I'm concerned about all the cats. Where will they go?"

Her parents shook their heads in unison. "Other shelters, probably," said Abby. "And not just the cats--what about your boss who's been working there for how many years?"

"She's been there ever since the shelter opened…five years. And she's adopted seventeen cats."

"Seventeen? Living with one is enough, right, Carson?" She stroked the now-resting cat who lazily twitched an ear in response.

"Point number two is to go for the interview tomorrow and see what happens. Don't let on that you work at the shelter or even know anything about it," Frederick said. "The cat shelter can't close without having a place to send the cats: namely other shelters. Plus, there are laws that prevent this kind of takeover."

"I figured that was the case. I also feel bad for the other workers and the volunteers who take such wonderful care of the cats."

Although the cat shelter was sixty miles away, up in Los Angeles County, it seemed like it was in another state. The sense of peace Yolanda got from sitting in the kitchen watching the seagulls wheeling through the sky and the palm trees caressed by the gentle breeze separated her from her daily reality.

It was February. The end of July wasn't that far away, and the welfare of all the animals was at stake.

"You know, dear, I was thinking about those cat treats you make…"

"Oh no, I forgot to bring Carson some. I was in such a hurry because of the interview!"

"That's okay; he's a chubby boy, and he gets plenty of treats, although he loves yours. But I was thinking maybe you can make them and sell them."

Abby reminded her of the nicely remodeled kitchen she had and how she could bake cat treats and sell them at pet stores and maybe market them to dog owners and sell them at dog boutiques and bakeries. Yolanda knew her mother had the best intentions but even if she wanted to, she couldn't. "Mom, I'd need a commercial kitchen and FDA approval. I couldn't do it at home."

Abby smiled. "Dear, I read an article in the paper about renting a commercial kitchen."

"Mom, it's a great idea, but it's not me. You know my dream. I've always envisioned a yummery maybe even with a café. It'll be a place where people come in and the amazing ambiance changes them--if only for a few minutes. The place is perfect from the pastel striped wallpaper to the large windows with frilly white curtains that are always open to the crystal chandeliers and the cute little old-fashioned ice cream parlor tables and chairs. I'll have cookies, brownies, cupcakes, and mini cakes. The boxes will be pink with yellow-and-green satin ribbons. Everything will be so good at Yolanda's Yummery. Super friendly employees who will treat everyone with respect…unlike that bakery where I used to work."

"I'm surprised you stayed there for so long," her dad said,

"You know me, I'm not a quitter. I mean, Hubert's Bakery in Studio City was so far behind the times. I was like twenty when I worked there."

"It was right around the time you moved into your grandparents' cottage."

"Right. First time living away from home, first full-time job." She got up to go to the fridge and opened it. "Hubert told me there was only one decorating tip to use on the cakes and cupcakes--the star tip. He refused to change anything. That's why he failed. That's why I won't."

She saw the glass bottle in the door and smiled as she pulled it out and set it on the counter. Yolanda admired the bottle of Oasis Creamery Organic Chocolate Milk. "Yum, my favorite."

Her mother got up and pulled a glass out of the nearby cupboard. "You and your father—chocolate fiends. I'm sure you see it's whole milk, not that two percent."

She watched as her mother poured a small glassful. "Thanks, Mom. You know what, I think Hubert was jealous of me because I found a bag of piping tips and used a large round tip. The cupcakes looked more sophisticated than the usual ruffled looking frosting. They sold out before closing time."

"I know, dear," Abby said, getting up. "I need to start making dinner." She walked over to the fridge.

Yolanda looked around, then stood up. "I left my purse in the car. Let me get it." She rushed out of the kitchen and down the hallway to the front door. Once outside, she went over to her car, opening the passenger's side door. Yolanda stored her purse beneath the seat, even when she was at her parents' house. Just as she grabbed it, she heard the telltale buzzing of new messages. Pulling out her phone, she saw that Zac texted twice about meeting at the movie theatre. "7:30 pm can u be here?" Noting the time on the phone and the sun's disappearing act was another clue that being in Burbank at seven-thirty wasn't feasible unless she hired a helicopter. Her response was brief, but it triggered an instant answer from him. She agreed to meet him at eight instead.

Returning her phone to her purse, she slid it beneath the seat and shut the door.

She heard footsteps and looked up to see her dad. He was holding a section of the newspaper. "You're not leaving, are you?"

"No, just checking messages. I'm going to see a movie tonight with Zac."

"Good, good." He walked over to her and folded the section in half, pointing out a picture. "Really good news, dear. A new baking supply store just opened up this weekend. It's near the Grove Shopping Center."

She leaned over and saw the photo and scanned the caption. "Yeah, It's on Fourth Street. Wow, that's so great. Thanks. Can I keep this?"

He chuckled. "That's the plan."

"I love the name--Sweet Spot Baking Supplies. I can't wait to check it out!"

Chapter 4

Yolanda rose before dawn to replenish the cat treats. The thought of making such stinky things day in and day out wasn't appealing, and the twice-weekly batches were enough to keep the shelter residents happy. The biggest problem lay with the impending job interview that evening. She couldn't reveal her almost three years of cat shelter experience—especially the cat shelter that was going to be liquidated that summer. Along with all the poor cats that couldn't get adopted...

That Monday morning, she walked inside the shelter and the thought of the place being turned into a Freeze N Bake storage facility was unimaginable. Some of the cats surrounded her with their greetings and she knew that they knew about the treats that were stashed in her tote bag.

Taking care of the cats was left to Laura, the only other employee to show up that hectic day. Front-office duties beckoned and between answering the phone, emails and keeping track of potential adoptees, she had no time for even a ten-minute lunch break. She was almost hungry enough to have a poultry treat or two. Missy neglected to phone her whereabouts, so at noon Yolanda gave her boss a call. She wondered if the woman was in a car accident or hospitalized. After the fourth ring Missy answered.

"Hello?" asked a groggy voice.

"Hey, Missy, just wondering if you're coming in today?"

Missy cleared her throat loudly. "Huh? I mean, what time is it?"

"It's noon," Yolanda said.

There was a loud clattering noise. "Noon! Oh, I'm so sorry, Yolanda. I'm getting up right..."

"It's okay, Missy."

"No, it's not. I've never overslept this long before. I'll explain as soon as I get there."

Missy showed up an hour later so that Yolanda was able to dole out treats to the caged felines. She spent an hour adding food to bowls and water to dishes and cleaning out litter boxes. Whenever she did that task the thought of being a bakery owner really sounded appealing, as the only aroma would be that of sweets punctuated with coffee, tea, and hot chocolate. But the thoughts of bakery bliss weren't long lasting, as she had to be on the west side of town by six o'clock for her second interview with Rocky. What would she do about mentioning her experience at the cat shelter? Maybe replace it with freelance baking for the past year or two? Or an intern at a bakery? No, that wouldn't be any good. Had Teagan mentioned her current place of employment? *I should text her and find out,* she thought, heading to the break room to grab her phone. Just as she was about to leave, the phone rang, and she ran over to answer it.

Holding down the fort and foregoing a lunch break would allow Yolanda to leave at five instead of six, especially as her boss had missed more than half a day. Missy rambled on about what had happened on Sunday night with the eighteenth cat to join the Wakefield household.

Having one cat was fine with Yolanda. The thought of having to deal with eighteen different personalities was daunting. She also knew that Missy's house smelled like the shelter and having to live with that odor all the time would have been Yolanda's undoing.

Just before she was about to leave, Yolanda went into the bathroom and changed into a pair of beige pants and a mahogany brown blouse. She'd leave her tote bag in the car and only take her purse. She thoroughly washed her hands with the bar of lavender-scented soap that was part of the private soap collection made by her friend Heather Hathaway. The powerful floral aroma rid her hands of any smell affiliated with cats. She left at five o'clock and was tense as she drove along the Sepulveda Pass through rush hour traffic. Fortunately, she was able to find a parking space only a block away from the Wicked Fun Gentlemen's Club and was on time for the interview. The same cashier sat at her station reading the free *Westside Weekly* magazine. She adjusted her red glasses and wordlessly picked up the phone, punching in Rocky's extension. After a minute, she got through to her boss. "Rocky—your six o'clock interview is here." She nodded.

"He said to go up to his office. You know where it is." The cashier reached over to the wall and pressed a switch. The sound of the door buzzer alerted her, and she thanked the cashier and went into the club. It was more hectic than yesterday and there were two dancers onstage. The same techno music was blaring over the speakers. Working in the main room was her friend Teagan, clad only in a tiny white corset that showed off her upper assets and barely-there bikini bottoms. As she bent over to serve a mojito swimming in lime slices and mint leaves, an elderly bald man with a blotchy red complexion stared up at her. He fanned out several twenty-dollar bills and shakily shoved them in her top. Yolanda waved at her friend but saw that the old guy with the money was what Teagan was focused on.

All Yolanda cared about was somehow preventing the cat shelter from being shut down.

Once upstairs, she saw the door was open; Rocky was sitting behind his paper-strewn desk. In front of him was a plate piled high with brownie squares. The chocolatey aroma was strong enough for her to detect standing in the doorway. Amidst the noise of the music and the stench of Rocky's strong cologne, she could smell that hyper-scent of chocolate flavoring. Did Rocky know that whatever was on that plate was masquerading as brownies? He had just finished eating a brownie; crumbs dotted a small napkin in front of him. Had he eaten more than one? "Hey, Yolanda, glad you're here on time. I like punctuality in my employees and my interviewees."

"Hey, Rocky! Thanks. I always try to be punctual."

He smiled at her, revealing chocolate-covered teeth. She hid a grimace and thought about how punctual she'd been working at the shelter. The place that would end up stocking those highly- preserved brownies.

"I'm testing these delicious brownies. Would you like to have one?"

She felt her stomach growl. Right around now she'd usually be having dinner in her dining room or sitting on the couch watching TV, using the coffee table to hold her dishes. "Thanks, I love brownies."

Yolanda walked over to the desk and saw about a dozen smallish brownies stacked on a plate. She reached for the top one and took a large bite. But her taste buds told her what she knew already: it was a processed brownie. There wasn't a smidgeon of butter in that batch and the chocolate flavoring nearly made her gag. It overcompensated for the fakery of the dessert.

"I can bake better brownies from scratch."

His thick eyebrows arched in surprise. "You can?"

She nodded, sniffing the square, observing it with all her senses. "First, mine contain real butter, not hydrogenated oils." She took a smaller bite and swallowed. "Mine don't have a chalky aftertaste, either. Using a high-quality bittersweet chocolate prevents that. Even the type of sugar makes a difference."

"How do you know this?"

"I love to bake. I also love cats. How can you sell out a cat shelter so you can store processed baked goods?"

"You know this how…?" Rocky paused and looked down at the stack of files pertaining to Freeze N Bake. "Oh, the letter you type for the test yesterday." He shook his head. "Are you with PETA?"

"Nope. I work at the Crown Street Cat Shelter. I've been there for almost three years."

He glanced up at her as she finished the last bite. "So, you don't want that shelter to close. And you don't want the agents of Freeze N Bake to buy it. You don't want to give more people jobs? You don't want to tear down that building and build a bigger, newer one that will give the community excellent fresh frozen products?"

"Hell no!" She crossed her arms over her chest. "Neither would any of the employees or volunteers. And especially not the 175 cats. Where will they go?"

Rocky shrugged and shifted in his chair. "I don't know. I'm a businessman." He raised his hands. "I own this fine establishment, and I also want to help my family improve a potential major corporation like Freeze N Bake. Get rid of cats and get rid of cat crap, is what I say. Who cares about a few stray cats?"

"I do. And I'm sure there are many more people who feel the same. Especially if I go to the media. People who love cats and animals might object to what you just said about getting rid of stray cats."

There was silence as they stared at each other. She looked down at the brownies. "I have an idea, Rocky."

He looked at her, and then at the brownies, which were her focal point. "What kind of idea?"

She began pacing. It was now nighttime, and the windows reflected her image as she walked and told the man about how she'd challenge Freeze N Bake in a public place with her brownies versus their brownies. Let the public decide who baked better brownies.

"So, you want to have my customers taste test brownies?" He laughed. "This is a gentlemen's club not a cooking show."

"I want anyone who loves desserts and cats and animals to taste my brownies--and compare them to Freeze N Bake's. We should have it at a public place."

He smiled. "I know…we can have it at the Planet Coffee Café over on Wilshire."

For the next fifteen minutes, they made arrangements. The event would be held next Saturday and they'd both do their utmost to promote the Great Brownie Taste-off.

Chapter 5

Yolanda's hectic day began right after dawn; she was going through all the dessert cookbooks her grandmother had left behind. She not only needed the perfect brownie recipe, but she also had to be able to make 400 of them on Friday—the day before the Great Brownie Taste-off. They had to be as fresh as possible, so she would make some trial batches to decide which was the best tasting as well as the least time-consuming. Going through her bake ware, she decided to buy a few more silicone pans and baking sheets to support them. She inventoried her ingredients and saw that she needed more baking chocolate. To save the cats, she had to bake the finest brownies imaginable, so she'd spend a few extra dollars. Her preferred brand of Valrhona, the Grand Cru Dark Baking Chocolate Guanaja 70%, wasn't sold just anywhere. Instead of the round morsel shapes, they were small oval-shaped bits, called *feves*, and worked best for melting. She knew that the type of chocolate she used was essential if she wanted to win the taste-off.

After entering the items she needed on her iPad, she pulled out her stash of cat treats and packaged them up for daily distribution.

Everyone showed up at work on time and Missy had even gotten enough sleep as the new cat, Prancer, was adjusting to sleeping on the living room couch along with several other feline companions with more seniority.

Just before lunchtime, Yolanda managed to talk to Missy in her office. Her boss's tiny desk was cluttered with paperwork and a few boxes and cans of cat food. Some banged-up cat carriers were stacked on top of each other in the corner.

A second after Yolanda sat down in the folding chair, Ozzie the office manager walked into the room and hoisted himself up on her lap. As she caressed his head and back, she rolled her eyes. "I don't think the office manager's losing any weight," Yolanda commented.

Missy grinned and pulled out a packet of diet cat treats. "Well, I guess pea protein, cranberries, and flaxseed aren't too high on his list of likes. And calling this Whittle Your Waistline is ridiculous. Cats don't have waistlines." She shook a few of the little green squares onto the edge of her desk. Had he felt compelled to eat any then he could have reached over and had a snack. All he did was glance at them, and then up at Missy.

"I think he's telling me that I must be joking." Missy chuckled and put them back into the packet. "Cats are like people--they know what kind of food they like and what they don't. Like me and cooked carrots."

"That's how I feel about cauliflower." Yolanda cringed. "I can give him some of my treats, but I can't reach them with him on my lap."

"I think he can wait for a treat until later this afternoon. So, how have you been doing?"

"I'm fine, Missy. Well, do you know if anyone's going to buy this building?"

"Buy this building? No, why?"

"You know that thing on Friday night with the message that was thrown at me? Like that was really weird, right?"

Missy shrugged. "Yeah, definitely weird. But like I said, this is a weird city. And nothing's happened since then."

Yolanda looked down at the scuffed floor. "Um, not exactly. Well, I've learned that by the end of July this place will be closed and turned into a Freeze N Bake facility."

Missy scowled and sat straighter in her wobbly armchair. "Why on earth would ... what are you saying?"

"Look, it's something I've just learned when I was, well, I went for a job interview on Sunday. My friend said I could earn $900 a day. You know how much I want my own bakery. I mean yummery."

"Yeah, so what does all this have to do with closing the shelter?"

"Turns out the job was at a gentlemen's club in West L.A. I couldn't strip but the owner thought I looked like a secretary and gave me a typing test. That's when I saw the letter about closing the shelter by July 31 and getting rid of the cats." She rubbed the cat's back, and he looked up at her questioningly.

Missy's mouth dropped open, and she gripped the armrests. "You're saying that this Freeze N Bake wants to get rid of the cats and open a facility here…of all places?"

"That's what I read, and what Rocky told me."

"Rocky who? Balboa?"

"No, Rocky Montoya." She didn't get the Rocky Balboa reference. "He owns the gentlemen's club and is also part of the family that owns Freeze N Bake."

Missy looked down at her desk and slid the chair forward, pulling out a manila folder. Opening it, she leafed through the papers. "I remember how a guy came here last month—or was it in December? No, I think it was in January. He was really interested in looking around. Not volunteering. Not in adopting a cat. He wanted to see…" She continued paging through the papers until she got to the last one. She shut the file and put it back where she found it. "No, I guess he didn't leave an invoice or any paperwork. But he said he worked for the county, and he had to inspect the shelter for a code. He gave me a long string of numbers and letters said some jargon; he seemed like an inspector or county worker. I can't remember his name. He wore a uniform—a gray uniform. Or was it tan? So maybe he was casing us out?"

"Sure sounds like it, Missy. And it reminds me of what happened last Friday. Just after I got here, I saw two men taking pictures. One had a camera the other a camcorder. They were across the street. That's why I didn't say anything -- because they weren't on the property. Then I thought that maybe they were taking pictures of the warehouse next door. But it seemed weird. So, I wonder if they're involved..."

She nodded. "Maybe. Wow, this really sucks. We can't lose the shelter."

"We won't. I've got a plan." Yolanda scooted her chair forward a little. Ozzie jerked and meowed at the sudden movement. "I want to tell you all about it so we can start making people aware of it and donating heavily. And eat brownies."

After discussing the Great Brownie Taste-off, Yolanda worked in the office and spent the rest of the day cleaning and feeding the shelter's inhabitants. As she was thinking of going to the new baking supply shop after work, she went to the caged area to distribute cat treats. Up in cage number 23, Mr. Whisker watched her intently, rubbing his sleek body against the bars and purring loudly. She approached him and stroked his body through the bars, then opened the cage to reach in and pet him. He purred even more and meowed softly as he nuzzled her hand. She gave him a few of the treats and he gobbled them down.

She left work a few minutes early to get a head start on her culinary shopping spree over the hill in the Fairfax district by CBS Studios.

Yolanda found the Sweet Spot Baking Supplies shop on Fourth Street. A large GRAND OPENING banner hung above the door. She eagerly entered the brightly lit shop, filled with a plethora of items bakers loved. The bright pink and chocolate brown motif made her smile as it was so appropriate. It reminded her of the reason for her visit, even though the selection of cupcake liners and piping bags and tips captured her attention.

Several customers were filling up shopping baskets and pushing small carts up and down the aisles. Yolanda eyed a display of colorful stand mixers and mixing bowls. Yolanda strolled down an aisle and added two copper baking pans to her basket and two bottles of Tahitian vanilla extract and vanilla bean paste. The organic bags of all-purpose flour were reasonably priced, as was the coconut sugar. The plastic basket grew heavier. Finally, she went to the last aisle and found the expansive chocolate section ranging from fondant to Swiss and French chocolate in bars, bricks, and bags. Her preferred brand wasn't available, but the large bag of Callebaut 54.5% semi-sweet caught her attention. She knew the high-quality chocolate was a little sweeter than the Valrhona but that didn't matter as she could add less sugar.

Just as she walked back down the aisle, she spotted the powdered cocoa. *Oh goodie, there's the Valrhona cocoa powder. Can't ever have too much of it,* she thought.

A jet-black-haired young woman wearing a magenta apron over a brown turtleneck and pants and holding a round rattan basket walked over to her. She reached into her basket and handed Yolanda a golden coupon. "Oh, I see you're a fan of our imported European chocolate! Me too! My name's Wanda Clark, and I'm the owner."

"Hey, I'm Yolanda Carter and I just love your store, Wanda. Thanks for the coupon," she glanced at the amount. "Ooh, twenty percent off, that's great news. I'm entering a brownie taste-off and I need the best ingredients. It's all about winning to save a cat shelter."

Wanda's smile widened. "That's so cool. I really support that because I love cats and dogs. My mom has a French bulldog and two Burmese cat brothers who follow her everywhere. Best of luck with your taste-off! When is it?"

"Thanks so much. I need all the luck I can get. Next Saturday at Planet Coffee Café."

"Cool, I'll be here but I'll be rooting for you!"

"Awesome. Will you be stocking the Valrhona feves?"

"Great question. Yes, they're on order but we won't be getting them until later this month. But I can call or text you when they arrive." The woman pulled out her phone and she and Yolanda exchanged their information.

***

At 7:30 she finally parked in her garage, unloaded her baking goods and her takeout bag containing a burrito and chips from her favorite Mexican restaurant. She went inside to see Miss Chef sitting in the dark kitchen waiting for her. The food and water bowls were empty and the way the cat sat there with her tail wrapped around her body made Yolanda feel guilty.

"Oh, I'm so sorry, Miss Chef. I was delayed. Let me get you a special treat."

First, she filled up the water bowl with some bottled water from the fridge. Then she went over to the cupboard and pulled out a small can of premium organic cat food that she only served occasionally so as not to spoil the cat. As soon as she scooped the meat into the bowl, Miss Chef was over there hungrily eating the late dinner.

She left her bags on the island and went to the sink to wash her hands. She hurried back into her bedroom to change her clothing to something not scented in eau de cat. After putting on a comfortable old sweatshirt and warm-up pants, she returned to the kitchen for her dinner. Flopping down on the couch, she put her tray on her faux Shabby Chic coffee table. Time to eat and watch a rerun of *Fancy Cakes.*

After her quick dinner, she put the dishes in the sink and began gathering her ingredients.

Pulling out the egg carton and two sticks of butter from the refrigerator, she set them on the countertop. *I must bake the best brownies to save the shelter,* she thought.

She'd baked two batches of brownies and when she tasted them, she wasn't sure which recipe to use, although she was leaning toward the one that contained organic coconut palm sugar instead of the brown-and-white sugar blend. She also enjoyed using the small round callets that melted faster and didn't need to be chopped up. The chocolate had just the right amount of flavor, neither too sweet nor too bitter. The brownies were also enhanced with some cocoa powder to make it extra chocolate-y. Tomorrow at work there would be some happy and hyper testers.

Much as she loved to bake, she also needed a hobby that didn't contain lots of calories and was relaxing. She went into her spare bedroom/office and pulled out her needle felting kit that her Aunt Margie had given her for Christmas. Opening it, Yolanda saw the miniature cat figure she was working on and felt the soft black alpaca fiber. Whenever she touched the alpaca or the colorful tufts of merino wool roving, it was soothing. She sat down at the desk, placing the foam mat on the area near the computer keyboard, and pulled out the container of felting needles. Lastly, she consulted the instruction book and for the next few minutes found a little escape in creating a small replica of Miss Chef.

Chapter 6

Yolanda set her alarm for seven, as she didn't have to get up before daybreak and bake anything. First, she'd test the brownies on her coworkers, and then she'd go to her parents' house and have them offer their opinions.

It was still dark outside, and she was lying on her side, her back to the clock on the night table. There was no light in her bedroom other than the glowing clock face. She always left her iPad in a kitchen drawer so she wouldn't be disturbed.

A pair of liver-spotted arthritic hands pushed a cookie-laden baking sheet into the oven. "Hurry up, old lady, hurry up. Those cookies must sell, hurry it up." The voice was haranguing. She turned and shuffled over to the worktable and scooped more cookie dough onto the baking sheets. She put the margarine, flour, sugar, and synthetic flavorings into the endless maw of the steel mixing bowl. She was numbly aware of the sameness of each batch. "Hurry up and be glad you can make cookies for us and increase our profit." There were clanging noises; other white uniformed employees, all old and hunched over, shuffling about the huge kitchen. An emaciated man dripping sweat pushed a stainless steel baking rack. The back of his wet shirt sported a large red-and-blue Freeze N Bake logo.

A red light flashed, and a siren punctuated the noise of the kitchen. "Oven three is overheating!" said the annoying voice. "Oven three needs attention now!"

She rushed over to the oven as fast as her orthopedic shoes would take her, the black smoke curling towards her, and she began to cough. She managed to insert her hands into the bulky oven mitts hanging from a nearby hook and pulled out a tray of burnt cookies. The invisible supervisor's voice said, "Put cherry-red icing on those--they can sell. Cherry red icing will cover up the burnt cookies."

Then she was back in her room, still in her bed, still only twenty-seven-years old, yet her heart raced with the hellish vision of her nightmare. Her heart rate gradually slowed down, and she became calmer. She fell back asleep.

That was when she saw the handsome black cat with the single white whisker. He sat on a satiny cushion and not in a cage. The cat rolled onto his side and started to purr. "Yolanda," he said. "I need a home." He winked and vanished.

Sitting up in bed, she looked at the clock to her right. 7:00. Time to check on her brownies.

She pulled the two pans of brownies out of the cabinet and was tempted to taste them but knew not to have that amount of sugar and caffeine as a breakfast treat. Avoiding her oatmeal-topped-with-sliced-banana breakfast and substituting it with a chocolate jolt meant she'd crave sweets for the rest of the day. She quickly placed the cut brownies into separate containers with different colored lids, so she'd know which had the coconut sugar and which had the brown and white sugar. Now it was time for a leisurely breakfast and mug of green tea with a generous spoonful of honey.

As soon as she went into the break room bearing the two containers, the cats were kept outside while Missy, Sid, Tatiana, and Julio followed her closely. "Obviously not cat treats – human treats!" Yolanda announced cheerily. "Only the daring need apply! I seek testers!"

Missy peered at the frosted plastic containers. "Those don't look like cupcakes."

"They're not. But I need people with picky palates! Pick your preference! I have two types of brownies here…" She reached over and set each container on the table. "Red lid, blue lid."

Everyone gathered in front of the brownies and looked at them. One batch was slightly darker than the other. "What's the difference?" Missy asked.

"Taste them and find out. I know they look almost the same."

Julio was the first to grab one from the blue side, only because he was standing closer to them. He took a large bite and sighed. "*Perfecto!*"

"Thank you!"

He nodded and gulped down the rest of the brownie. "*Muy perfecto.*"

"Okay, now tell me what you think of the other batch," Yolanda said.

Julio reached over and took one from the red side. He bit into it and concentrated as he chewed the sweet chocolate. He smiled and finished the brownie. "*Perfecto.*"

Everyone laughed, Yolanda the hardest. "Thanks, Julio; that really helps me."

Sid took the brownie test, starting with the blue side. He took smaller bites and closed his eyes as he focused on the tasting. Taking a sip from his water bottle, he declared. "I'm clearing my palate now. Okay, time for the red brownie." With an equal amount of deliberation, he ate that brownie. Finally, he pointed to the blue container. "We have a winner. I don't know what's different, it just tastes richer."

Tatiana and Missy tasted both and one chose the red and the other opted for the blue.

"Okay, I'll tell you what the difference is. Red side is white and brown sugar, blue side is coconut palm sugar."

"I wish I had time to bake," Missy said.

Yolanda laughed. "I wish I had *more* time to bake."

She covered the containers and stacked them on top of each other. "I'm going to store these in the cabinet below the coffee maker till I go home. Then I have to test them out on one more person; if you have any that's fine, just leave about two or three of them."

"We will, Yolanda." Tatiana smiled. "I like both red and blue but maybe red a little better."

"Thanks, Tatiana."

Yolanda's morning consisted of working in the office uploading photos of new cats. The rest of the time was spent taking care of adoptions. A man wearing round glasses and dark coveralls sidled up to her and smiled. "I'm looking for a male black cat."

"We have a few of those. Let me show you."

She led him back to the caged area and saw that all the cages were full except for number 23. The black cat she had dreamt about was gone! He'd been there this morning when she walked by on her way to the office. "Oh, yes, in number 15 we have Jackson. He's only two years old and used to live with a family until the mother was diagnosed with allergies."

The man looked at the cat. "Nah, too scrawny. I need me a big cat. A strong and muscular cat. I like 'em big." He smiled even more as he scrutinized her from head to toe, lingering on her chest for several seconds. Licking his thin lips, he repeated himself. "Yep, I like 'em big."

She looked at him and saw the name Leo on his red and white badge. "Well, Leo, these are our current adoptable cats. We update our website daily with new arrivals."

Leo looked at the rest of the cats with a cursory glance. "Nope, none of these will do. I like 'em big and black, if you know what I mean." He stood closer to her. "You like cats?"

"No, I prefer iguanas; that's why I work at a cat shelter."

"So, do you live around these parts, miss. What's your name?"

Just then, Sid made his six-foot-plus presence known. "Hey Yolanda, I was told that our staff meeting begins in five minutes and you gotta attend. Maybe I can help this gentleman?"

The man looked up at Sid and saw the scowl on his young face. "Um, no thanks, that's okay. I'll check out your website tomorrow..." He turned and almost ran down the hallway and out the front door.

"Sid, thank you so much! That skeezy slimeball was really freaking me out. I don't ever want to be around him again. And make sure that he never adopts a cat from here. Tell Missy about him."

"Done." He saluted.

"You were kidding about a meeting, right?"

"Yeah…not till tomorrow."

"Okay, fine. Have you seen the cat that was in number 23?"

They both look up at the cage. The muscular black cat was sitting on his haunches and cleaning his front paw. Yolanda turned and stared at Sid. "I guess I missed him…"

Sid nodded. "Yeah, he's a little small and hard to miss." He burst out laughing and walked away. "April Fool's Day is in two months."

The cat winked at her.

"Okay, I can take a hint. You're coming home with me."

That evening, instead of unloading her two almost-empty brownie containers from the car, Yolanda had an even larger receptacle: a borrowed cat carrier. Miss Chef was sitting in the kitchen doorway awaiting Yolanda's arrival—something she usually did when the cat knew a special kind of food was imminent. Only, this special arrival would also demand cat food. Yolanda pulled out the carrier, gently setting it down on the garage floor. Mr. Whisker meowed softly. "It's okay. I want to welcome you to your new home properly. I'm going to unload my bag and brownies first and set up a food and water bowl just for you. Then you'll meet Miss Chef, your new roommate. She's looking forward to meeting you."

Once inside, Yolanda checked the tux's food and water bowls and filled them up. She found two clean bowls and added a combination of standard cat chow mixed with some of her homemade treats. Handing some treats to Miss Chef, the cat eagerly gulped them down. She poured water from the fridge into the second bowl.

Returning to the garage, she picked up the carrier, closed the garage door, and went inside. By now, there was a lot of loud meowing emanating from the carrier. Miss Chef stopped eating, went over to the strange new resident, and growled.

"Miss Chef, this is Mr. Whisker. Please don't growl at him. He needs a new home. I told him that you're very friendly."

Miss Chef's ears flattened, and her tail swished as she growled at the newcomer. Yolanda sighed and thought, *I'd hoped this wouldn't happen—but I figured it would.* "Okay, Miss Chef, let's go into my room. Mr. Whisker, I'll be right with you."

The irritated tux stared at Yolanda and then went back to looking at the feline trespasser and growled with gusto. She edged closer and began batting at the male with her right paw.

"Now Miss Chef, I thought you had better manners." Yolanda picked up the irritated tux and carried the cat into her bedroom, depositing a few treats on the rim of exposed hardwood floor in front of her closet. The cat went for them. An instant later the door was closed, and Yolanda returned to the kitchen. She unlatched the carrier's door and Mr. Whisker stepped out. He looked larger when he wasn't in a cage, and he rubbed himself against her legs and purred. She reached down to stroke his head and then picked him up, hugging him. "Welcome home, Mr. Whisker."

There was a loud knock at the back door, and she put the cat down. She went over and opened it, seeing Zac standing there in his golfing attire. Yolanda stepped aside for him, and they greeted each other with a kiss and hug. Zac walked in, closing the door behind him, and looked around. "Hey babe, what's for dinner?"

Mr. Whisker suddenly left the kitchen and Yolanda noticed he went right for the couch. Soon she'd have to show him the location of the litter box.

"Hey, Zac, I have some lemon chicken that just needs to go in the oven. It should be ready in about twenty minutes."

"Crap, I'm really hungry. Can't you like nuke it in the microwave?"

"No, I rarely use it these days. Oven-heated chicken tastes much better."

He rolled his eyes. "Whatever. I had to deal with so many idiots today you wouldn't believe it. Some Tiger Woods-wannabe takes a swing at the ball on the 14th hole, you know the one with 20-foot waterfall? So anyway, this guy takes his putter and swings it like a baseball bat. I mean who does he think he is? So, he ends up almost hitting my boss. I mean, it just misses Eddie's head."

"Wow, he's lucky he didn't get hit."

"Nah, he's always lucky like that. We also had a group of a dozen douchebags who were like doing some sorta business meeting. They were wearing suits and trying to pretend like it was a PGA tour or something. One of the guys kept saying he wanted to bring his golf bag with him. Then he wanted to know where the golf carts were."

She smiled as she went over to the fridge and took out the casserole dish. She put it in the oven and set the temperature and time. "You always have funny customers."

"I know. I should write down the stories of weirdoes I've met at Green Palms. It'd be a best seller."

Yolanda chuckled. Then she pointed out the two different brownie containers. "I bet it would be. Would you like to compare two brownies for the Great Brownie Taste-off?"

"What's the Great Brownie Taste-off?"

"Well, I'm raising money to save the cat shelter from being bought out by Freeze N Bake. I'm baking brownies and the people who own Freeze N Bake are baking brownies. Whoever has the best brownies wins and if we win, we keep the shelter."

He went over to the red-topped container. "And if they win?"

"No more cat shelter. But they won't win."

"Well, that sucks. You'll be out of a job."

"I can find another job. I'm worried about the cats' finding homes."

Zac bit into his brownie. "Freeze N Bake brownies are pretty good...."

The scowl she gave him caused him to swallow quickly. "But not as good as yours. With brownies like these you'll win." He finished it and went over to the fridge to pull out the milk container, taking a quick swig. He paused and put it back fast, letting the door close. "What the hell kind of milk is that?"

"Coconut milk. I like it because it has a longer shelf life and it's easier to digest. I have real milk behind it."

He opened the door and looked inside, finding the whole milk and taking a swig. "Thanks, that's better."

"So, did you like the brownie?"

"You know I do. I like whatever you bake."

"Thanks. Now try the other brownie." She offered him one from the blue-topped container.

He gulped it down in one bite. "It's good."

She put her hands on her hips. "Zac, you can't taste anything different from the first brownie?"

He shook his head and went back to the fridge. She cut in front of him, grabbed the milk bottle, and set it down on the island. "Here, I'll get you a glass." She walked over to a cupboard and pulled out a glass edged with frosted turquoise—one of her father's unique creations. She poured the milk into it and set it down, sliding the full glass over to him. Zac downed most of the contents.

"Darn, I didn't realize how thirsty I was. I like both brownies. I can't taste a difference."

She returned the milk container to the refrigerator and let the door close behind her. "Well, I thought you might detect something in the flavor..."

"They're both winners." He finished his milk.

The cuckoo clock chimed seven times. Zac jumped, startled by the sudden interruption. He watched the cuckoo peeking in and out of the small door, announcing the hour along with accompanying gong sounds. When the little bird was done and returned behind the door, on the platform below, two pairs of dancers wearing dirndls and lederhosen spun around to the tinny rendition of "Edelweiss." He rolled his eyes after the top-of-the-hour show ended. "That's so lame. Hey, when's the Taste-off?"

"Next Saturday from one to three."

"You're joking."

"No, why?"

He folded his arms and glared at her. "Why? It's only the biggest day of the year for me. The 25th Annual Green Palms Mini Golf Tournament—the one I've won every year ever since I was nineteen years old? You know, the biggest event …"

"Oh Zac, I'm so sorry. How could I have forgotten?"

"I guess you don't care if I win or lose, not that I'll lose. I thought my girlfriend would be there to cheer me on."

"What time does it start?"

"It's from ten to five."

"I'm sure I can make it by four o'clock." Yolanda said as she moved closer to him.

He shook his head. "Not the way I planned it. I want my girlfriend wearing a sexy outfit and being there the entire time to cheer me on. I want you to kiss my putter for good luck. I want…"

There was the sound of frantic scratching and yowling noises coming from her bedroom. She raced out of the kitchen and into her room followed closely by Zac. "I hope Miss Chef's all right," she said as she dashed inside. The cat was rolled up in one of the sheer bed drapes. "Hold it, Miss Chef, I'll get you!" She knelt and touched the lumpy area where the cat was desperately rolling and scratching. After a minute, the cat calmed down and began purring, though still stuck in the jumble of lightweight fabric. Yolanda carefully removed the claws and soon untangled the cat. "Looks like we're having a dining companion." Looking at the fallen drape, she noted the amount of damage was minimal as there were only a few small tears.

When they returned to the kitchen, Mr. Whisker was sitting in front of the oven staring at the glass door. Yolanda said, "I think we'll be having two dinner companions tonight."

"I'm not hungry," Zac said. "All you care about is baking and cats. You don't ever show up at my golf course. Now you won't be there to cheer me on."

"Zac, I'd love to go there on Saturday. But if I can save the shelter…"

"Good luck. I'll pick up a something at the store." He rushed out of her kitchen.

The door slammed behind him. Seconds later, the revving of his engine terrified Mr. Whisker, who bolted into the living room and hid beneath the sofa.

"Oh great, now the cat's freaked out. Thanks, Zac."

The car backed out of her driveway and tires screeched loudly as he turned onto the street. He cranked up his radio and the loud bass-heavy music startled Miss Chef who ran back towards the bedroom.

Yolanda stared at the kitchen window; glad the noise was fading as the car sped away. "Why is he my boyfriend?" She looked at the oven. "He seems to get more immature the longer I know him."

Chapter 7

The Great Brownie Taste-off was a week away. She would bake 400 brownies. Since she was a perfectionist, those 400 brownies would be baked the day before the event so they would be fresh, and because the representatives from Freeze N Bake would also bake their brownies on Friday.

Yolanda received her chocolate *feves*, they had shipped perfectly, not a melted one in the bag. The temptation to start making the brownies was strong, but all she could do was make sure she wrote out the recipe and had changed the amounts of ingredients correctly.

Mr. Whisker was adapting nicely to being a house cat and Miss Chef was spending her days outside in the fenced-in backyard, and her evenings in the living room or in Yolanda's bedroom. Mr. Whisker enjoyed sitting on the couch and napping or watching cooking shows. She knew he didn't miss being stuck inside a cage all the time. He also enjoyed sitting on the windowsill in the living room and watching the activity outside.

Tonight, she was meeting her good friend Heather Hathaway in her new Larchmont area home. Yolanda phoned in the order for takeout dinner just as she exited the Hollywood Freeway.

Yolanda swung by the Wok Express. Once inside the small restaurant, she was pleased to pick up her order without waiting. She left a generous tip in the inevitable tip jar next to the cash register and touched the golden lucky cat statue with the raised right paw. *I need all the good luck I can get*, she thought, and thanked the young cashier.

A few minutes later she drove up the driveway in front of a two-story Spanish-Mediterranean villa that was three times larger than her cottage. Just as she and the two bags emerged from the car, a woman with strawberry-blonde hair, wearing an elegant ivory suit and aqua kitten-heels, appeared. Her hair was rolled into a sleek bun, so she resembled a ballet dancer, an effect enhanced by her slender figure. She rushed up to Yolanda and hugged her.

"Hey, Yo, I missed you!"

"I missed you too, Heather. I've got some great news, but first I wanna hear all about your vacation in Maine."

They pulled away and Heather looked at the bags. "Thanks so much for getting dinner. I'll pay you for it."

"No, it's my treat."

Yolanda followed her friend up the flagstone walkway and into the house.

"Look, I need to change out of this costume. I'll be right back. Help yourself to anything to drink."

The palatial Hancock Park home that Heather and her husband, Barry, had recently moved into was a foreclosure. The previous occupants were involved in shady dealings that landed them in a tiny, locked prison cell. The house they left behind wasn't on the market for more than an hour when investment broker Barry Hathaway finagled a deal. The couple had difficulty keeping up with the mortgage payments.

Yolanda noticed the gleaming hardwood floors, and each room was entered beneath wide arched doorways. The sparsely furnished living room only had one colorful Mexican rug. A fresh bundle of logs sat on the grate in the fireplace.

One of the selling points was the chef's kitchen with the six-burner Wolf range. Heather could make scrumptious omelets and was adept at boiling water for Ramen noodles, but the reason she needed a deluxe stovetop was her business: Heather Hathaway's Lotions & More. Heather made body lotions and creams from scratch; a feat that struck Yolanda as marvelous. What she did with baking,

Heather did with natural plant oils, nut butters, and floral essences. She was always a willing tester and couldn't remember the last time she'd bought a conventional brand of lotion or even a bar of soap.

Heather hurried downstairs and into the dining room. Her hair fell in loose waves midway down her back and her faded jeans were roomy as was her pink sweatshirt. "I'll get the dinnerware," she called out as she dashed into the kitchen. She returned bearing two cobalt-blue plates. "Vintage Fiestaware! I got it at a moving sale in West Hollywood last month. It's amazing what you can find if you know what to look for. The whole dinner set was like ten bucks!"

She set the plates down on the wooden table. "Yeah, I know, I need to get a real dining table that matches this place. Even if it's secondhand. But for now…"

"It's fine; I like it."

"Nah, the wood looks cheap and doesn't match at all. I have to resort to using tablecloths when we have business dinners. But the good news is that next week we'll be renting out the apartment above the garage so that'll help with the bills."

"So, it's completely self-contained back there?"

"Yeah. There's even a washer and dryer so it'll be nice for whoever rents it. Very private. It'll be extra money for me and Barry."

Heather pulled out the containers and smiled. "I just love how Chinese food smells!" She opened them and passed one to Yolanda, along with chopsticks and extra soy sauce.

Yolanda emptied half of the contents onto her plate. "I usually eat this as is, but I must try out your new plate."

"Everything tastes better on it. But this orange chicken would taste great on a paper plate." She laughed. "It rhymes; I need to make a wish." She paused and then dove into her meal, expertly plucking chunks of chicken with the bamboo chopsticks.

Yolanda speared a shrimp and a bit of scrambled egg and ate quickly. "Heather, I wanna hear all about your vacation."

"Well, it was so wonderful to not see any smog, or hear traffic noises. But it was so cold! I didn't even pack a winter coat, so I had to buy one there. But it was cool 'cause I got to go to LL Bean."

"I'm jealous," Yolanda said, scooping up some rice with her chopsticks, wishing she had a fork instead.

"The best part of it, I mean aside from spending time alone with Barry for almost five whole days and nights, was the idea I came up with for my fall product line. Get this -- Nautical Nor'easter! It'll be a line of lotions with a tangy ocean scent and with blueberry seed oil. Blueberries are full of antioxidants."

"Sounds like a working vacation, Heather."

"Is there any other kind? Even Barry met a potential new client while we were walking along the beach."

"That's great. So, what are you doing next Saturday?"

"Probably making more lotion samples. Why?"

"Would you like to attend the Great Brownie Taste-off?"

Yolanda told her friend about the forthcoming event and Heather immediately took to the idea. She brought out her laptop. "Let me share it on my social media pages." She entered in some words and paused. "Wait, I'll need some brownie photos from you."

"Not a problem. I have some test brownies left over, and as soon as I get home, I'll take pictures and send them to you."

Yolanda looked at the leftover shrimp fried rice on her plate and scraped it back into the carton. "I never can finish the whole thing," she said, closing the lid.

"I know what you mean. Barry will devour it when he gets back later." She returned her orange chicken to the container and then looked in the bag. "We forgot the egg rolls and the fortune cookies!"

"Keep 'em," Yolanda said.

"You sure?" Her friend reached into the bag and pulled out three fortune cookies. "I think you should have a fortune cookie—there's one for me and you and Barry." She handed her one.

"Okay, thanks."

"Thank you. I'm just so happy about the Great Brownie Taste-off. I think it'll be a huge success. Especially for such a worthy cause."

Yolanda tore open the wrapper. Cracking open the cookie, she pulled out the slip of paper. "Heather, it says 'Among the lucky, you are the chosen one.' Yeah, right!" On the reverse side were six numbers: 06 23 29 32 39 42. She saw a vision of Mr. Whisker winking at her. She shook her head and looked at the numbers again. She was born on June 23—maybe that was a good sign. She pocketed the fortune and quickly ate the cookie. "What does yours say, Heather?"

Heather opened hers and chuckled. "It says the same thing—we're both the chosen one!"

"Or two. Whatever. Well, I gotta go home and take some pictures."

Chapter 8

The day before the big event, Yolanda didn't bring treats to work as she was taking Friday off so she could bake the 400 brownies.

She calculated the number of batches she had to make, and, before sunrise, she was in the kitchen along with her two kitty cat helpers. A morning of baking awaited her.

Yolanda selected her favorite pink flowered apron and as she tied the strings around her waist, the importance of what was at stake made her pause. "I need to bake the best ever brownies, so that I can save the shelter." She was doing a task she loved and doing it by herself meant that she was honestly taking part in the taste-off. Only her two cat friends were assisting by sleeping on the floor near the living room. After the first batch was done, they got bored and retreated to the sofa. She scored the brownies before cutting them with her pizza cutter, and then set out all the lidded plastic containers that she had in the cupboards. At the event, they would be transferred to the glass-covered pedestal cake stands that her father had made.

Recounting the brownies as she sliced them and put them into the containers, she discovered an extra dozen. In between batches, she breakfasted on a banana and a slice of whole-wheat toast slathered with butter, so she was only mildly hungry as she bit into one of her freshly baked brownies. It was still warm from the oven, and intense buttery chocolate hit her taste buds with an explosion of flavors. The complexity of the imported chocolate was evident.

At first, it was a decent home-baked brownie. But the more she chewed, the textures and flavors flowing in her mouth, the less she wanted to swallow it. She didn't want to drink milk or water or anything to drive away the intense flavor and the goodliness that pervaded her as she took another bite. As she slowly relished the brownie, she stared at the refrigerator and was pulled into a vision of where she was on the beach. To her left was a pier—Santa Monica? Malibu? She wasn't sure, but she saw a man wearing navy blue trunks that emphasized his tanned skin and muscular chest. His hair had natural golden highlights. Piercing eyes caught her attention. Behind him, the surf crashed against the shoreline and the seagulls soared overhead. There was no one else on the beach; it was only the two of them, both drawn to each other … their eyes focused on one another.

And then she was standing in her kitchen, looking at the refrigerator. *That's strange*, she thought.

Just then, Miss Chef pranced into the kitchen followed by her new brother, Mr. Whisker. Yolanda greeted them, and bent down, stroking their backs. She sat on the floor and leaned over, picking up the tuxedo and kissing her on the top of her head. "I guess you want your lunch now." She got up and went over to the cabinet and pulled out a can of tuna fish, opened the lid and evenly divided it into their matching bowls. Mr. Whisker winked at her. That made her smile as she watched the cats devouring their treat.

Checking her phone, she saw there were two missed calls: her mother and a hang up. She'd call her mother later as she decided to drive to the Planet Coffee Café to check out the situation there. It was something she'd planned to do but kept getting sidetracked. Stacking all the brownie-filled containers in the top shelf of the pantry, she went to her room to change into something more suitable than her apron and old sweats.

She opened her closet door and peered inside. Flipping the hangers from left to right, she coordinated an ensemble of violet and black sweater and a slim skirt, paired with sensible sandals.

After a quick shower, she finished the contents of a bottle of tropical coconut and lime scented body lotion. She rubbed it on her skin like a layer of sheer silk. The perky aroma enhanced her happy state of mind brought on by baking such yummy brownies. She knew they'd be featured on her yummery menu.

Traffic on the Sepulveda Pass was typically only a bit faster than the 405. Since it was a bright Friday afternoon, she noticed more convertibles. Zac would be on the mini golf course training for his big event. His BMW would be roofless today. She remembered how he'd stormed out of her house because she couldn't attend his golf tournament. But worse than that was the fact that he scared Mr. Whisker on his first night in his new home. The poor cat was so upset by the noise of the car that he stayed under the sofa for several hours.

For once, she found rock star parking right in front of the coffee shop. To her delight, thirty minutes remained on the parking meter. As she approached the front door, she was pleased to see a sign advertising the Great Brownie Taste-off from 1 – 3 PM on Saturday. Seeing the words *Donations will go to help save the Crown Street Cat Shelter* made her grin with relief. Until she saw that Freeze N Bake was also supporting animals. *Donations will go to help build the new Rocky Montoya Dog Rescue Mission in Ojai, California.*

Inside the café, the aroma of percolating coffee awakened her sense of smell, along with the happy accompanying scents of cinnamon, chocolate, sugar, and earthy spices. Music consisted of intermittent parrot and monkey calls, along with a steady backbeat of drumming and rainfall noises: an imitation of the rainforest. Vivid colored macramé holders supported an array of hanging plants. Potted palm trees and coffee bushes enhanced the natural greenery. She thought the foliage of the coffee plants was clever, highlighting where the popular beverage originated.

Beneath the skylight was a two-story high waterfall, tumbling over rocks. The sight and sound of the impressive cascade further enhanced the illusion of an indoor jungle.

Yolanda sighed when seeing a broad-shouldered man of barely legal drinking age. She made her way between the little tables crowded with a variety of caffeine addicts.

The only place where the taste-off could be held was near the bar area unless the tables were moved elsewhere. Yolanda went to the other side of the café to see if there was a patio or courtyard or another room. She saw nothing to indicate that and went to the coffee bar to scope out the action. Sitting on a padded stool, she studied the chalkboard menu that spanned the width of space above the bar. She wondered how often it was changed and admired the neat printing. Enough sugar and caffeine coursed through her system, so she decided to get something neutral. Noticing a dessert section on the menu, she got up and went over to the large glass case filled with a tempting array of cookies, doughnuts, pastries, croissants, and brownies.

Hmmmn, brownies. Looks like it's time to do a little taste test, she thought as she went back over to the stool and sat down.

"Hey, how're you doing?" she greeted the barista.

He leaned closer to the countertop and gave her the twice over—slowly and sensuously. She reveled in the feeling of being studied by him and stifled a giggle. Warmth spread from him to her and intensified when he spoke. "You're looking very thirsty."

His cheesy line was correct. Then again, if she weren't thirsty, she wouldn't be there. "I'd like a mineral water with a twist of lemon and a plain brownie," she said.

He beamed back at her. "Hmmmm, you seem like the type who'd like a steamy hot chocolate topped with whipped cream, because you want to mix hot and cold."

She giggled. "Maybe you're right."

He nodded. "And maybe you'd like a cherry on top of the cream?" He licked his lips, and she noticed his tongue and the full lips that curved in a knowing smile.

"That's okay, I..."

"You know, I'm not just a barista. My name's Bradley and I've been accepted at UCLA's Anderson School of Management. But that doesn't mean I'm no fun." He leaned closer to her, and she smelled his intoxicating cologne.

"I've gotta warn you, I'm a good girl."

His smile broadened. "Yeah, but all bad girls start out as good girls."

"That may be true. But I still prefer to have a mineral water with my brownie." She smiled sweetly at the flirtatious man.

"But of course. I'll be right back." He scurried off, returning a moment later with an iced glass filled with the sparkly water. A sliver of lemon floated on the surface. He stuck a straw in the glass and presented it to her. Before she could thank him, he hurried over to the pastry section, took a sheet of wax tissue paper, and grabbed a brownie, putting it on a small plate.

When he returned, her smile was still there, and she wished her sweater was cut lower and that she'd bought it in a smaller size. "Um, thanks. But I was wondering..." She looked at the brownie and gently touched it. Way too dry. Ugh, how old was it? "Do you bake these here?"

His high wattage smile dimmed. "I'm afraid not, miss. They bake them in El Monte and send them to us."

"Oh, I see," Yolanda said, looking at him and then back at the perfectly square brownie.

He handed her a fork and a napkin.

"You know, the company Freeze N Bake is sponsoring a taste-off tomorrow afternoon. Right here, from one to three."

She ran the fork across the top, hearing a scraping sound. "Oh cool, I saw the sign for it."

"Yeah, Freeze N Bake makes really great brownies. And their cookies are almost as good as, um, romance, if you know what I mean…" The wattage in his smile was back.

Yolanda knew not to show her amusement mixed with the derision for the Freeze N Bake line of products. "I've never tried one," she said, trying to push away the memory of that one she'd eaten in Rocky Montoya's office.

"Bradley, you've got a call on line three!" a young barista said as she put two large cups on a tray.

"Excuse me," he said, and rushed to the other end of the café.

She continued studying the Freeze N Bake brownie. Cutting off a small corner took a bit of effort. How old was the thing? A quick sniff revealed a cloying aroma of artificial vanilla flavoring and cheap chocolate. Reluctantly, she took a small bite, and the lack of butter was immediately apparent since hydrogenated oils were used to extend the shelf life. It tasted just like a commercial brownie that had been left on the supermarket shelf well past the end date. She looked up and saw the price on the menu and shook her head. Far too much money for such a synthetic dessert. *They should change their name to Freeze N Fake*, she thought.

A slight thump to her right caused her to look up. She saw a laptop being placed upon the granite countertop. A thin man with shoulder length hair the color of caramel sat down next to her. She couldn't help noticing his eyes matched his blue T-shirt. He gave her a quick once over as though trying not to be obvious, and then focused on the brownie in front of her. "You like brownies?"

"Sure." She was about to tell him that she adored desserts and had been baking them since receiving her first Easy-Bake Oven twenty years ago. But she just laughed instead. "Actually, I love brownies and cookies and cakes..."

He chuckled. "You've got a real sweet tooth."

"I've always loved sweets. When I was a kid, I'd be rewarded whenever I got an A in school. I made sure I got all A's, so I got more sweets that way."

The young man wasn't even looking at his computer but staring at her intently. "My name's Patrick Stewart..." he began.

Laughing hard, she leaned forward and covered her mouth for a few seconds. "That's funny," she commented when she resumed breathing normally. "You've got hair and you're American."

"I know." He flipped up the lid of his laptop; she saw a bold burgundy-and-black header that read *The Other Patrick Stewart*. A caricature of the guy sitting next to her emphasized the fact that it was indeed his blog.

"I see you like to blog. But are you an actor, Patrick Stewart?" she asked, appreciating the way his faded jeans clung to his legs.

"Not anymore."

"You used to act?"

"When I was a child. I had what you call a stage mother. An extremely ambitious stage mother. And my last name had to be spelled differently because of SAG rules, meaning there could only be one Patrick Stewart, so my last name was spelled Stuart. I only did minor TV roles and bit movie parts. I remember my last part the most: a commercial for Bucket Fried Chicken Wings. I spit out the chicken wing at my costar and walked off the set. After the forty-eighth take, I decided that was way too much and left. I realized how much I hated commercials. And fried chicken."

A young barista with flaming crimson hair that matched her tank top hurried over to Patrick. "Hey, Pat, how's it goin'?"

He offered her an even longer appraisal, focusing mainly on her abundant cleavage as he smiled exclusively at her. "Now that you're here it's goin' beautifully, babe…"

That was Yolanda's cue to leave a nice tip for the handsome barista and book it back to her place. She recalled Zac's temper tantrum. It was nice to flirt with other men. It made her realize that there were other prospects. She swallowed the fizzy water to drown out the unappealing brownie. A squirt of lemon obliterated the chalky aftertaste. She left a hefty tip on the counter and slid off the stool. "Nice meeting you," she said to Patrick.

He looked over at her for an instant, giving her a dazzling smile, then looked back at the red-haired barista.

With only eight minutes left on the parking meter, she pulled out and drove onto a side street that led to Olympic Boulevard. A few blocks later, she saw a 7-Eleven food store and went inside to buy a lottery ticket and fill out the numbers that she'd found on the back of the fortune. She shoved the lottery ticket into a smaller compartment in her wallet and returned it to her purse. Even though the other brownies didn't taste as fresh as hers, what if people didn't care and decided to vote for the Freeze N Bake team anyway? Would it come down to a battle of the cat shelter versus the dog shelter?

Chapter 9

Yolanda sat on a folding chair behind a rickety table that looked like it was about to collapse. The people at the Planet Coffee Café were ignoring the pink plates containing her brownies. The other table was festooned with red velvet and staffed by bikini-clad women, including Teagan. Only a few brownies sat on the blue plates. Men were hanging around stuffing bills into the bikinis and the women were strutting about in their stilettos and handing out plates of brownies in exchange for twenty-dollar bills. A raven-haired woman was sitting on the lap of an old man, and he was showering her with twenties and fifties. A large donations box was brimming with so much money that a second one had been added, placed there by Bradley, the handsome young barista who had served Yolanda.

Zac strolled into the café and started dancing with a perky golden-blonde exotic dancer, tucking twenties into her bikini bottom. He was handed a brownie by another nubile employee of the strip club, and she fed him the brownie as she danced behind him. Zac boogied with the exotic dancers and enjoyed a Freeze N Bake brownie as he doled out money to them.

The small shoebox that she had hoped to fill was almost empty. Neat rows of brochures and business cards were untouched. Beneath the table sat her unopened plastic containers still filled with brownies. Her parents were hanging out on the other side of the café and her dad was chasing after a stripper while her mother stuffed herself with the Freeze N Bake brownies, declaring them to be delicious. Heather had set up a lotion and soap display and several people lined up to try samples and buy her products.

A man in coveralls was holding a piece of notebook paper that read YOU LOSE!

The front doors to Planet Coffee Café crashed open and dozens of cats raced inside followed by men in grey uniforms. Mr. Whisker was cornered and yowled when a man tried shoving him into a cage.

Yolanda awoke from her nightmare to the sight of Mr. Whisker and Miss Chef wrestling with each other at the bottom of her bed. She sat up, her heart pounding hard, her nightgown sweaty. The cavorting cats set her at ease—at least they were safe. But what if that nightmare was a sign of impending failure? What would happen to all the cats?

She couldn't adopt any more, nor could Missy. Sid wasn't allowed to have any pets in his apartment. Laura had too many birds. Tatiana loved cats but her cranky German shepherd was the king of the household. Julio already had five and his wife wouldn't let him adopt another.

It was eight o'clock and she had to leave no later than 11:30 if she wanted to get everything set up in time. The main event of saving the cat shelter was top priority. She could also help her parents with their coordinating efforts: her father's glass cake stands and her mother's batik T-shirts and tank tops with cat designs. Yolanda had stayed up until the wee hours of the morning creating a photomontage of the shelter's cats and kittens. She packed up dozens of brochures, business cards, adoption forms, and her booklet of kitten-and-cat tips.

Yolanda chose a bohemian-splendor outfit of a long cotton skirt in yellow, topped with an aqua and magenta blouse. The wide silk headband matched the skirt.

Peeking in a full-length door mirror, she did a quick spin. Her feline roommates admired her, and if they thought about using her as a climbing tower, which didn't happen as she was soon out of the house and into the garage.

She pulled the car up in front of the back door so it would be easier to load. The most fragile items were the hand-blown glass cake stands that were covered in bubble wrap and blankets and boxed separately. They were delicate and heavy, but she knew the addition of them on any kind of table would enhance the class factor.

Missy and her husband would oversee the pet adoption area outside Planet Coffee Café. Two dozen cats and kittens would be on the premises for immediate adoption.

Heather arrived in time to help finish loading the car and the last items were the four brownie-filled containers.

Their drive time was less than thirty minutes, but they had to circle the block in search of a parking spot. Heather emerged from the car and went into the café, returning a few minutes later with a big smile. "Dwight the manager says you can park in the loading zone while we get everything out of the car."

Entering Planet Coffee Café and seeing the vacant area in the back reserved for the taste-off made her grin. Freeze N Bake's GREAT BROWNIE TASTE-OFF, read the appropriately chocolate-brown-and-sky-blue banner above the two long tables. She noticed they were regular folding tables. Neither of them looked rickety; even if they did, she was prepared. A trio of plain chairs sat behind each of the tables. Looking around, she noticed that she was the first participant to arrive. Maybe Freeze N Bake and the Wicked Fun Gentlemen's Club wouldn't bother showing up and she'd win by default.

Heather moved quickly back and forth between the car and the table. Picking up the last box, she hurried across the café and was followed by Yolanda's parents, who were also carrying bulky boxes.

They began unpacking the glass pedestal cake stands. The skylight emitted sunshine and the glassware sparkled. Abby took a cloth and polished them so there were no smudge marks anywhere. She lined the bottom of each one with a paper doily.

Outside on the sidewalk, Missy and Roger Wakefield along with Sid, Julio and Laura, had finished loading the cages showing off cats and kittens. A small crowd had gathered, and a young couple was admiring a half-grown tabby.

Yolanda walked over to greet her boss and Roger. The couple sported matching logoed Crown Street Cat Shelter sweatshirts. She greeted them and looked at the adoptable cats in separate cages. "So glad to see you. Hi Roger, wonderful that you're helping out."

"I wouldn't miss this big event," he said. "I hope these cute kitties all go to happy forever homes today."

"Me too!" Yolanda strolled over to the last cage. "Oh…I see Cameo's here!" She bent down and touched the calico through the bars. "I sure hope she finds her forever home!"

"That makes three of us," said Missy.

"I certainly hope so. Well, off I go. Almost time!" Yolanda turned and left.

Everything on Yolanda's side of the café was ready for the start of the Great Brownie Taste-off. The table was covered with a lacy white tablecloth. Brownies were artfully arranged on each of the cake stands, some with transparent glass, others with swirls of bright colors. Stacks of pink paper plates and matching napkins sat next to each of the four displays. In the center was the donation box, decorated in kitty-cat wrapping paper and above it featured the poster board showing many of the adoptable felines. On the other side of the donation's box was a line of booklets informing the public about the Crown Street Cat Shelter. Folded multicolored batik T-shirts and tank tops with cat-themed designs were offered. A "FREE WITH $20 DONATION" placard sat next to them.

The other table had been moved farther away and it was covered with a plastic zebra-striped tablecloth. A sign announced the Rocky Montoya Dog Rescue Mission in garish red letters. HELP US BUILD! Beside the donation box was a pixilated photo of a gray-and-brown mutt with its head cocked to one side and a smaller picture of a bulldog. "YOUR DONATIONS WILL SUPPORT BUILDING OUR SHELTER."

Melanie, a tank-top-wearing, coffee shop employee, carried out a small table and set it between the competitors' tables. On top of it was a large cardboard VOTE! box with a slot cut into the top. Two stacks of pink-and-blue squares of paper were set out. The job of the young employee would entail adding a color-coded paper that corresponded with the brownie that the entrant preferred. As soon as she saw the setup, Yolanda hoped that many pink squares would go into the box.

A somberly suited Rocky Montoya swiftly entered and went to the table to oversee the setup. A pair of men wearing lab coats with the Freeze N Bake logo embroidered on the chest, marched in carrying covered trays of brownies. The skinnier man wearing glasses went up to Rocky and announced, "We are the creative brownie baking team."

Missy rushed over to the men. She pointed at the one who had just addressed Rocky. "You, you were the one who was at the shelter spying on us."

The man looked at her with a smile that didn't reach his eyes. "I did no such thing."

"Yes, you did," Missy said, staring at the man. "That shelter won't ever be yours." She turned and strode out of the building.

Rocky shrugged his shoulders. "I apologize. I don't know what that's about. But, please, put your brownies over here." The men placed their trays on the table. Rocky looked at the doorway. He waved, rushing over to the main entrance, and escorted three of his scantily clad employees into the café amidst a mixed reaction of cheers, whistles, and lots of stares. Teagan brought up the rear of the line. Her silver stilettos glittered as she strutted towards the table.

"This is a coffee shop not a strip club," commented a woman to her friend, who nodded vigorously in agreement.

At Yolanda's table, her father was staring at the exotic dancers. He was part of the majority, going by some of the slack-jawed patrons of various ages.

The café was getting more crowded. Dwight, the manager, walked up to the middle table promptly at one o'clock. The atmospheric jungle music stopped. He picked up a cordless microphone, tapping it gently. "Good afternoon, everyone. Welcome to Planet Coffee Café's first ever Great Brownie Taste-off sponsored by the Wicked Fun Gentlemen's Club and Freeze N Bake!"

There was applause from the gathering of employees and customers in the café. The sound increased as the exotic dancers in their tank tops, featuring a glittery white silhouette image of a stripper on a pole, sashayed up to the podium and stood next to Dwight. He grinned as the

Wicked Fun Gentlemen's Club employees surrounded him. The young man snuck a glance down the top of a particularly buxom woman. Melanie had been shoved aside. She glared at her boss. Rocky stepped over and stood on the other side of his girls.

Yolanda was standing near her brownie display with her mouth open. "Mom, they didn't even mention the cat shelter!" Abby nudged her, and Yolanda went over to the gathering near the center table.

Dwight smiled as he raised and lowered his hands and the noise of the crowd diminished.

"This unique Great Brownie Taste-off will help support two charities that are dedicated to helping animals in need!"

Audience applause increased, and it was Yolanda's turn to step up to the center table.

"I'm going to hand the mic over to Yolanda Carter, a dedicated employee of the Crown Street Cat Shelter and the baker of brownies."

Yolanda nervously accepted the mic and looked around at the large gathering of people. "Um, hey, my name's Yolanda Carter, and..." a burst of feedback crackled over the speakers, and she stopped talking. She looked over at Dwight and he mimed holding the mic closer to her mouth. She thought he was making a dirty gesture and almost dropped it. The downward movement caused more howling noises from the mic. Several audience members held their ears.

"Hold the mic closer to your mouth," Dwight said loudly.

There was a lot of laughter. Yolanda's face reddened, but she obeyed and held the mic closer to her mouth. "Um, I work at the Crown Street Cat Shelter." She tried to keep the shakiness from her voice.

There was a smattering of applause from the supporters at her table.

"I'm here to help save the shelter from being sold to the Freeze N Bake Corporation." She cleared her throat and looked around anxiously. "Um, I baked these brownies to raise funds to help save..."

"Where's your tank top?" asked a shaggy-haired man.

"Yeah, you're wearing too many clothes," said another guy.

"I'm here to help raise money to save the cat shelter. The more you donate the more you can help save cats and kittens from being homeless. And if you want to adopt a cat today, we have several outside the café that need good forever homes."

Her parents and friends applauded, as did a few people in the audience. "I've baked these brownies to help our furry friends. If you like the brownies, please vote by adding a pink piece of paper to the voting box."

Dwight picked up the box and held it up over his head. There was some clapping. Yolanda returned the mic to Dwight after he replaced the voting box on the table.

"You hear that, people? Vote for Yolanda's brownies and donate generously to help save the Crown Street Cat Shelter. And now, Mr. Rocky Montoya, owner of the Wicked Fun Gentlemen's Club has brought along this trio of lovely ladies to help you try the magnificent brownies from Freeze N Bake! And don't forget, this is all to help raise funds to support the building of his Rocky Montoya Dog Rescue Mission! Now take it away, Rocky!" Dwight gave Rocky the mic.

Rocky accepted it, as his posture straightened, and his smile was genuine. "People, Freeze N Bake makes great brownies! In fact, the Wicked Fun Gentlemen's Club is teaming up with them because of that. We'll be serving them in our club. Or should I say, the Wicked Fun Wanton Women will be!"

Many of the attendees began applauding and cheering.

Rocky held up his free hand so the noise could abate. "But the most important thing, besides the great brownies, is the homeless dogs that need a home. Everyone knows that dogs are man's best friend!"

A few people barked like dogs.

Applause filled the air. Several of the people laughed at the noise of barking.

Rocky held up his free hand again, and the barking ceased. "And I, Rocky Montoya, will see that your donations for the Rocky Montoya Dog Rescue Mission will be well spent!"

Hearty applause and cheers were heard, along with more barking sounds. The skimpily clad dancers bounced up and down and were shimmying about, increasing the noise as they played to the audience.

Yolanda stood there, staring at the show of excitement.

Teagan saw her, and for an instant the dancer stopped moving and she frowned at Yolanda.

Yolanda was taken aback, her jaw dropped as her friend tossed her head back and resumed her task of jumping around to entertain the audience.

Wow, Teagan's job has really gone to her head, she thought.

Rocky waved the mic back and forth, as he barked along with the pumped-up crowd. Dwight stepped over and reached for the mic. Rocky stopped barking and paused, reluctantly returning it. Then he stepped over to the dancing girls and made a quick stop gesture by jerking his hand in front of his throat. His smile disappeared.

The dancers abruptly stopped. Dwight went to the side of the table and pointed to the box. "Okay, people, it's time to chow down on some delicious brownies. On one side is the easy-to-make and easy-to-love Freeze N Bake's brownies. Vote with the blue square if you choose them. Remember, by eating them you support a fine company and help save the dogs." He picked up a blue square of paper and held it up.

Applause and barks resounded around the café. Dwight cleared his throat. "Okay, on the other side, the girly pink side, are the brownies baked by Yolanda Carter of the Crown Street Cat Shelter. If you like hers, vote pink and save the pussy … cats!" He went to the box and picked up a pink square amidst the applause and laughter.

Teagan and her coworkers began setting brownies on the blue plates and a line of eager testers immediately formed. Abby went over to the line to buy a brownie and returned to the table with it. Yolanda took a bite and was surprised to taste a homemade type of brownie—it wasn't made with artificial flavoring and hydrogenated cottonseed or canola oils, it was made with butter. It didn't taste like the other two Freeze N Bake brownies she'd sampled.

Patrick Stewart approached Yolanda's table and was joined by Louie, his videographer.

"Fans, this is the Other Patrick Stewart. I'm at the Planet Coffee Café for the first-ever Great Brownie Taste-off. I'm having so much fun and am going to eat some brownies. I understand you're the talented young lady who baked all these brownies to save the shelter. What's your name?"

"I'm Yolanda Carter and I want you to meet my parents, Frederick and Abby Carter. I also have my best friend, Heather Hathaway, here to support saving the Crown Street Cat Shelter. And my boss, Missy Wakefield, is outside with some adorable cats and kittens that can be adopted today!"

She reached down to pick up a plate and hand it to Patrick. "I use only pasture-range local eggs and the butter comes from a dairy farm in Pomona. I use French chocolate and the brownies are my own recipe."

"I've just tasted Freeze N Bake's and they're quite good." Patrick glanced over at the people crowding the other table. "I see they're getting tasted a lot." He winked.

Yolanda grinned and watched as he bit into a brownie. "I've noticed."

"Very nice," Patrick mumbled, as his mouth was still full. He paused and took another bite. He chewed and closed his eyes. He continued chewing, his face relaxed, and he almost dropped his mic. He plopped the remaining brownie into his mouth as he grinned, standing motionless, only his mouth moving as he tasted the magnificent dessert. Patrick stepped closer to her. He stopped himself, straightened up, and looked away from her and at the camera's unblinking red eye.

"I'm back at Planet Coffee Café with Yolanda Carter who works at the Crown Street Cat Shelter. This young lady also bakes the most amazingly awesome brownies I've ever tasted. When I was chewing, I never wanted to stop. Even now I don't want to drink coffee or milk or even water because that would detract from the taste. In fact, I've got such a chocolate buzz going on that I don't want to stop!" He extended the mic near Yolanda. "Please tell me your secret to these incredible brownies!"

Yolanda smiled radiantly at the reporter. "Fresh and high-quality ingredients for one. And I believe in the total love and magic of baking."

"Well, you have some magical brownies. The best I've ever tasted."

The reporter's glowing praise of Yolanda's brownies had brought over several curious people. Money was pushed into the gift-wrapped donations box as the pink plates topped with the brownies were distributed by her parents and friend. Yolanda kept the lid off one of the cake stands as she carefully plated each baked chocolate goodie using a glove to protect them.

A bewigged senior citizen stood over to the side, admiring the cake stands. "I've been looking for a new cake stand," she said. She fell into a conversation with Frederick as she munched on a brownie. "It's hand-blown Borosilicate glass. I prefer to use this type of glass because it's not so heavy, and it's even dishwasher safe." Perhaps that sentence sealed the deal because the woman ordered two pedestal cake stands and felt quite obligated to donate twenty dollars to save the shelter. She beamed when she was told to select a T-shirt or tank top.

Rocky and his sexy employees still had a few spectators, including a lanky man in overalls and a beige baseball cap. He picked up a blue plate and sniffed the brownie, then crammed the whole thing into his mouth, eating noisily as he marched over to Yolanda's area.

He threw the paper plate at her and pointed. "Oo loo, oo loo." He said, his cheeks bulging as he incoherently addressed the baker.

"Excuse me, sir?" said Frederick, staring at the rude younger man. "Didn't your mother teach you not to talk with your mouth full?"

"Oo loo," the man repeated, pointing at Yolanda.

She paused, looking carefully at the gibberish-spouting man. "You lose? Is that what you're trying to say?"

He nodded vigorously and turned and ran out of the café. She stood there and watched him leave; her mouth open.

"What an incredibly rude man. His picture should be in the dictionary next to the word loser."

"I think he was the one who told me and Missy to get out."

"What on earth are you talking about, dear?"

"I'll tell you later, dad. Let's win this taste-off so we can save the shelter. That's what really matters."

Holding hands, a young sunglass-wearing couple radiated confidence and familiarity; they were known as the Knick Knacks, a modern-day version of Sonny and Cher. Their current hit, "Can I Trust You?" was many a teenager's anthem. Knick was the singer, guitarist and songwriter and Knack wrote the songs. She also had a stronger singing voice than her boyfriend. The one-hundred-dollar bill they stuck into the box caused a wave of happiness among Yolanda's crew. Abby thanked them and offered the couple two batik T-shirts. They received their brownies and ate them at warp speed. The woman stood for a full minute, staring at a cake stand, and admired the brownies it contained. "It's not that I don't want a second brownie, because I do, but I don't feel the need to have another one. This one is perfect the way it is—it's filling enough. And I don't want the wonderful flavor to go away."

That was the common sentiment. Heather enjoyed the attention her friend's dessert was garnering. She encouraged everyone within earshot to eat a brownie and donate generously.

A man with a graying comb-over stood next to the table after sampling a brownie and stared at his cell phone. "Gotta call Tammy and tell her why I broke up with her last year," he said to himself as he hunted for the phone number in his directory.

Two ladies wearing black yoga attire sat at a table, drinking coffee and eating Yolanda's brownies. One of them burst into a fit of giggles. "Bryan saw me at the Westside Pavilion yesterday and couldn't get over how good I looked since I lost almost fifty pounds. Now he wants to get back together with me. I don't trust him after he cheated on me. But the main thing is, I've met Alan and he's my soul mate."

Slipping a pink square into the box, a tall Black man in dress slacks and shirt ambled over to donate. As he reached for his wallet, he addressed Yolanda.

"Best brownie I ever ate," he said.

"Thank you so much. I'm so glad you liked it."

He shook his head and fumbled in his billfold for money. "But the darndest thing happened to me. I've been mad all week. Now I'm not. And I can't even remember why I was so mad!" He pulled out a fifty-dollar bill and put it into the box. "Maybe you should call this brownie therapy!"

"That's a great idea—brownie therapy! Thank you so much for your donation, sir. Would you like a T-shirt or a tank top?" Abby asked.

He looked at the few remaining T-shirts and pointed to a pink one. "My daughter loves anything pink."

Abby smiled. "So does mine." She handed him a T-shirt and he thanked her and walked out of the café with a big smile.

Missy and her husband dashed in at two o'clock, asking for more brochures and flyers to distribute.

"Cameo might have a forever home. A nice man said he'd be back by three, Missy said.

"That's great," replied Yolanda, giving Missy and her husband each a brownie. "First thing I've eaten today," said Missy, devouring the brownie in two bites. The couple left, hand in hand.

Yolanda's brownies were all gone fifteen minutes before the bake-off officially ended. The last to be served was a five-year-old boy who wore a baseball cap and shorts outfit. He lifted the khaki fabric to show his cut-and-swollen knee. "I fell off my bike," he said. "It's a big two-wheeler."

"Oh, honey, I'm so sorry to hear that." She handed him a brownie. "This'll make you feel better."

He accepted the brownie and eagerly ate it, licking his fingers after he finished it. "Thanks, I feel better now!"

His mother approached, holding the hand of a little girl. "I wanna brownie," the little girl shrieked.

"I wish we still had some brownies, sweetheart, but we just ran out. I think they have some left over there." She pointed to the other table where a few dozen brownies sat on blue plates.

"Let's go over there and get your sister a brownie."

A bearded man wearing a white-and-navy yacht cap and captain's jacket staggered inside and over to Yolanda's table. Noticing the cat pictures, he pointed a beefy finger at the donations box. "Too many cats I say! They've taken over the internet. Soon they'll take over the world."

Yolanda smiled. "Rocky and his friends are trying to build a dog shelter. Maybe you can help them out."

The man stopped, looked over to his right, and noticed the gentlemen's club employees and the plates of brownies. He weaved over to the table and waved his arms above his head like a captain aboard a ship spotting land. "Strippers and brownies – wow-wee!"

At three o'clock, Dwight stepped up to the mic and announced, "The Great Brownie Taste-off is officially over. I want to thank everyone for making this such an enjoyable and extremely tasty event! We'll now count the entries and announce a winner within the next few minutes."

He picked up the box and carried it to his office behind the coffee bar. Melanie followed him. Yolanda and Rocky grabbed their respective donation boxes and walked over to the manager's office behind the bar so that the tallies and donations could be counted.

Yolanda looked around the cramped office and stayed near the doorway just after Dwight closed it. "I want to thank everyone for their participation," Dwight said. "What I'd like to do is count the pink and blue votes to see who the winner is. Please watch Melanie and I do this. Then, you can count your money as soon as we're done so that we can announce the winners and the total amount raised for the charities."

Melanie and Dwight opened the box and started pulling out each square of pink and blue paper. "I'm going to tabulate each blue one and Melanie will count each pink one. We'll use our own calculators."

Yolanda and Rocky were silent as they watched the counting. They stared anxiously as the seated Planet Coffee Café employees quickly removed each piece of paper. Blue, blue, pink, two more blues, the squares of paper slipped from hand to table. Yolanda leaned forward to see the small calculator's numbers but couldn't since they were held closely by each user. She counted every bit of pastel pink that traveled from box to desktop and that color looked like it was in the majority until a flurry of sky-blue ones appeared. The last dozen seemed to alternate between pinks and blues. Dwight and Melanie posted the final two and there was a long pause as they totaled the amounts.

Dwight and Melanie wheeled their chairs close together and peered at each other's calculators. He wrote the numbers down on a sheet of paper and studied his again, as though affirming the number to himself. "We have a winner. We'll announce it to everyone along with the money totals. You'll each need to count your money."

"Who won?" Yolanda asked.

"Yes, I'd like to know before everyone else," Rocky said.

The red-shirted duo exchanged lingering glances. Dwight smiled, as did Melanie. "I understand. But as soon as you finish counting your money then we can go out and announce the winner."

"Okay," Yolanda said, lifting the lid off the cat-motif-wrapped box. She began sorting out the bills by denomination. She paused, seeing so much money, genuinely pleased that people were supporting the cats and her baking. The faster she counted, the sooner the results would be known.

Rocky didn't reflect on anything other than the fact that he was seeing a lot of green bills and they needed to be counted pronto. It was something he'd been doing for years. Five minutes later he had his total. "You want me to tell you how much is here now?"

"You mean as opposed to later?" Dwight chuckled. "Just kidding, man. Yeah, let us know."

Rocky's face reddened and he scowled. "I'm sure I'm the winner. We made $10,337.80."

Yolanda nodded. "You won. We made less than you did. We made $9,124.55."

Rocky smiled and shook her hand. "Congratulations, well done."

"Thank you and congratulations." Yolanda said.

Dwight was the first to stand up. "All right, we have the numbers, and we have the results. Let's not make anyone wait any longer."

"I agree," Yolanda said.

"So do I," Rocky said, as he allowed Dwight and the ladies to go ahead of him.

Dwight was holding the box and the two stacks of colored paper squares, along with his sheet of paper where the totals were written. He led the way back to the main room of the café, stepped behind the small table, and set the box down on it. The drumming music that was playing during the counting intermission stopped. Interested parties at both tables focused on the manager. The spectators stopped talking. A barista quickly served a customer, and then stood aside and focused on her boss.

Patrick and Louie, his cameraperson, stood front and center. Dwight cleared his throat. "Now that the Great Brownie Taste-off is officially over, I again want to thank the Crown Street Cat Shelter, Freeze N Bake, and the Wicked Fun Gentlemen's Club…"

A loud chorus of applause and hoots interrupted the speech. Teagan was jumping up and down causing a stir among many of the men. Rocky was grinning at her and applauding her enthusiasm.

Dwight was captivated by the floorshow for a few seconds, and then resumed his duties. "And I think the Wicked Fun Gentlemen's Club has some very fun ladies working there. I'm happy to announce that they have raised $10,337.80 to help finance the building of the Rocky Montoya Dog Rescue Mission in Ojai, California."

More applause from the audience, especially fans of the strip club. Some of the guys barked.

Yolanda politely clapped but she kept looking over at her parents and supporters. She nervously clutched the moneybox and waited for Dwight to announce her total.

"Coming in at a close second, many of you have contributed $9,124.55 to help the Crown Street Cat Shelter."

A swell of clapping and cheering was heard from the cat lovers and supporters in attendance. Her parents and those affiliated with the shelter stood in a close-knit group next to their table.

Dwight held up his hand for silence. The big moment that everyone was awaiting involved the taste-off – who had the better brownies? Yolanda clutched the box harder and watched the red-shirted manager. He studied the numbers on the paper in front of him. "We have a definite winner with a large lead, showing that people prefer the home-baked brownies of Yolanda Carter! The final score is Yolanda and the Crown Street Cat Shelter with 324 votes, Freeze N Bake, and the Wicked Fun Gentlemen's Club with 291. Congratulations to the winner!"

Shouts and cheers filled the room and Yolanda's parents rushed up and hugged her. Heather followed Yolanda's coworkers. Sid, Julio and Laura rushed over. Yolanda hugged her parents and cried. "My brownies were good enough...I didn't think they would be. I was so scared we'd lose the shelter." She began crying and Abby was wiping away her own tears, as was Frederick.

"I'm so happy for you," Heather said.

Yolanda sobbed with relief and Missy went over and congratulated her. She looked up to see Patrick approaching.

"Congratulations on winning the Great Brownie Taste-off, Yolanda! Can you tell the viewers what this means to you?"

Yolanda wiped away the tears with the back of her hand and nodded. "It means that we've saved the Crown Street Cat Shelter from being bought out by Freeze N Bake."

"It means she makes the best darn brownies in the world," Abby announced loudly. "My girl has always been a great baker, and now this proves it."

"She's an awesome pastry chef," Heather chimed in. "Her cakes and cupcakes are super awesome and then some!"

"Thank you so much, Heather. I appreciate all your support."

The three exotic dancers were no longer animatedly bopping around. Teagan looked nervously at her boss, as did the other two women.

Rocky stepped closer to Yolanda, and as she felt the sensation of winning engulfing her, he stepped over and shook her hand. The exuberant showman she'd seen at the start of the taste-off had vanished, replaced by a man with a chilly demeanor. He leaned over and whispered in her ear, "We know the shelter's barely getting by. If it goes out of business, I won't be violating any laws if we buy out the property." Rocky bared his teeth, and his eyes were flat and cold. An acrid odor emanated from him, like cheap cologne gone bad.

Shocked, she pulled away from the club owner. Patrick had seen the exchange and furrowed his brow as Yolanda's expression changed from elated to worried.

***

Around dusk, Yolanda drove into her garage and unloaded the car. Her two feline friends were eagerly awaiting her return. She received many figure eights wending around her ankles, and the purr meters on both registered in the upper volume level. "Hi, Miss Chef. Hi Mr. Whisker. Hope you were well-behaved today. We raised enough money for your shelter friends." The approving purrs revved up, along with some enthusiastic meows.

She went to the cabinet to get their food and decided they both needed hard-and-soft dinners mixed up with her homemade cheddar cheese-and-chicken treats.

Yolanda set her purse on the counter, removed her cell phone, and checked for messages. Zac still hadn't called her. No emails, texts, or voicemails. He'd known about the Taste-off, but she knew he was more concerned about his tournament, which lasted until five o'clock. She hit his stored number and got his standard voicemail message. "Hey Zac, I hope you won the tournament today. Good news…I won the taste-off and raised over $9,100. Call me."

She went out to the garage to get her cake stands and containers that needed washing. Her father was right about the glass stands being dishwasher safe. However, only two were able to go in there and the others had to be hand-washed along with the plastic storage containers. Looking in the fridge, she didn't feel like cooking or even warming anything up. She saw a magnet on the front of her refrigerator for Antonio's Pizzeria and decided to order a pizza and garlic bread sticks. She went into the living room, sat down on the couch next to her now-sleeping cats, and pondered her future.

The donations the shelter had received today would temporarily help, that was true. But she knew there would always be more cats and kittens arriving at the shelter. What about her job there? Inputting cat descriptions on the website and cleaning litter boxes wasn't what she longed to do with her life. Neither was earning a barely livable wage. Working at a strip club office paid more, as would almost any other office career, but it was as far from baking as her current job. What about working at another bakery? Having to be told what ingredients to use? Using shortening instead of butter and cheap flavor oils and watered-down vanilla extract? Making the same cookies and cakes every day?

The doorbell rang, and she grabbed some money from the drawer in the coffee table where she kept some cash reserved for food deliveries.

Yolanda rushed over to the front door and looked through the peephole before opening it. Bathed in the bright porch light wasn't the expected uniformed pizza-delivery person. There stood Zac. He held a single red rose wrapped in cellophane in one hand and in the other was a large trophy. She smiled and yanked open the door.

"Yo, sorry I wasn't there to see you win. I was on my way over here and just got your message and want to congratulate you. I also wanted you to know that I won the tournament today." Zac proudly brandished the trophy with a golf figure in mid-putt posed on top of it.

"Congratulations, Zac!" She moved aside to let him enter the living room. He set the trophy down on the front hall table. As soon as she shut the door behind them, he swooped in for a kiss and she responded. He pulled her closer to him and they stood, kissing passionately. Seconds later, the doorbell rang. They quickly broke apart. "Ooops, I guess that's the pizza!" She was still holding the money, he was still holding the flower, and they both chuckled.

Yolanda opened the door and there stood a teenager wearing a green baseball cap and matching shirt. "Small margherita pizza and garlic bread sticks order for Yolanda Carter?"

"That's me!" She offered him the money in exchange for the cardboard box.

"Great." He told her the amount.

She accepted her dinner and as he reached into his pocket, she shook her head. "Thanks for being so speedy. Keep the change."

"Awesome! Thanks dude!" He turned and ran down the walkway back to his waiting car.

"Hey dude, can I get a piece?" Zac asked her.

"Maybe." She went into the kitchen, and he followed closely behind.

"Your flower, mademoiselle," he said, offering the wrapped rose.

"Thank you, monsieur." She smiled and took a whiff. "It smells beautiful." She admired it for a few seconds. "Now I must put it in water." She went to the end of the hallway where a white plant stand decorated the alcove outside her bedroom. An elongated vase held a fake orchid. She removed it and went to the kitchen where she added water to it. Peeling away the cellophane, she put the rose into the vase. "Okay, you can serve the pizza though if I'd known you were coming over, I would have ordered a large pepperoni and sausage."

Against the dining-room wall stood the breakfront china cabinet that displayed some Wedgwood plates and Easter egg ornaments, along with her father's more colorful plates and glasses, all highlighted by soft lighting and a mirrored back. There were three drawers below the shelving and on each side were two small doors. Yolanda sat on the floor while opening one of the doors, as her grandparents' small wine collection was kept there. She pulled out a bottle of Chianti that had last been used in a beef recipe she prepared around Christmastime. After a wild-and-crazy twenty-first birthday fiasco where she was given several free drinks in several different bars and bistros, she had spent the next day regretting each bottle and glass of booze she imbibed. Yolanda preferred soft drinks. What went better with pizza than a bottle of icy cold root beer?

She pulled two plates out of the cabinet and placed them on the linen covered table. A pair of wine glasses rimmed with jade green enhanced the beauty of the formal setting. Zac placed his trophy on the table as a centerpiece. As they sat down to dinner, Mr. Whisker amused himself by sharpening his claws on Zac's pants and then sat on his lap and purred. As soon as Zac placed the cat on the floor, he jumped back onto the man's lap. Yolanda allowed it to happen twice and then took Mr. Whisker into her bedroom and closed the door. "He either likes me a lot or he's guarding you," Zac said as he dunked a breadstick into a container of marinara sauce.

Miss Chef sat on the dining room chair to Yolanda's right and was so well behaved that she fell asleep almost right away. Zac and Yolanda quickly ate and discussed the day's events.

The cuckoo clock called out once and Zac dropped his breadstick. "Yikes, that thing always makes me jump." He looked at his watch. "Hey, it's 7:30; let's check out the sports segment. I was interviewed just after I won."

They moved over to the couch, and she switched on the TV. Channel 12's local news was in progress. After a series of commercials, most of them offering bargains for juicy cheeseburgers or touting endless amounts of beer, the sports segment aired. The panning shot revealed the colorful Green Palms Mini Golf Course with the large windmill, tall palm trees, and quaint Tudor-style buildings. There were shots of people holding neon-orange golf clubs and wearing the casual attire of T-shirts and shorts, hitting neon-orange golf balls around water traps. Several scenes showed balls driven into the mouth of a shark. A girl in shorts and a crop top expertly hit a ball--and it landed with a plop onto a sandy island.

"They're not showing the tournament. This's the usual TV commercial footage," Zac said.

There was a slow motion shot of Zac as he made a hole in one. Behind him, the windmill churned. The sportscaster was an older man with an orangey-red toupee that revealed sparse silver hair fluttering around his ears in the wind. He clutched his mic and began his patter. "Good afternoon, Channel 12 viewers. This is Vern Hess filling in for Mike Griffith. I'm here at the Green Palms Mini Golf Course in Toluca Lake and we're here to..." He noticed a spectator standing very close to him.

A teen in a T-shirt advertising a popular band stared at him. "Whoa, dude, is that a bird's nest on your head?"

Zac and Yolanda burst out laughing.

"You're a putz," Vern said and walked over to Zac. "Tell me young man, isn't a putt-putt golf tournament a joke?"

Zac straightened up and stared at the sportscaster. "It's miniature golf—not putt-putt."

The sportscaster chuckled. "Where I'm from, viewers, it's called putt-putt." He pointed to the windmill and the camera operator zoomed in on it. "You don't see windmills at Augusta or Pebble Beach."

Quickly the image on the screen changed and focused on Zac, holding the large trophy above his head and grinning. A young blonde in a tiny black miniskirt and top went up to him and wrapped herself around him, kissing him aggressively. They were lip-locked and neither looked like they wanted to stop anytime soon.

"Hey kids, there's a Motel 6 down the street," Vern quipped.

Yolanda picked up the remote control and turned off the TV. "What the hell was that all about?"

"Yo, I didn't even know the bimbo. She just came up to me and -- she attacked me!"

"Yeah, right. I think I've seen enough." Yolanda stood up and glared at him. She went over to the dining room table and picked up the plates, stacking them on top of each other.

"Okay, okay I can take a hint. But I didn't do anything. It was just a joke."

Yolanda carried the plates into the kitchen and put them in the sink. "If that's a joke, it's not very funny. Not funny at all." She pulled up the chrome- sprayer attachment on the sink and flipped on the water. As he approached her, Yolanda directed the stream of water at his chest, soaking his golf shirt.

Zac stood there with his hands in front of him, wetting them in the process. "Stop it!"

"Just trying to cool you off. Maybe you should go back to your bimbo. Good-bye." She turned off the water and put the sprayer back in place.

"You mean, good night."

"No, I mean good-bye," she said.

He quickly left and she slammed the door behind him. Just as she was about to get the glasses from the dining room table, she heard loud pounding on the back door. She turned to see Zac in the driveway. He yelled, "Hey, I need my trophy!"

Chapter 10

The image of Zac kissing that younger woman haunted her as she slept restlessly that night. She realized that Zac hadn't been a supportive boyfriend, and he was larger and stronger and could have pushed the immature fan away from him. But he didn't. So, he was to blame. Both cats kept her company, and she wished she could sleep as soundly as they did. Just before sunrise, she finally fell asleep, and awakened a few hours later as groggily as if she hadn't gotten any rest.

She got up and fed the cats, letting them go into the fenced-in backyard. Yolanda wanted to sleep the day away. Instead, she made herself a cup of rooibos tea and some instant oatmeal. After a quick shower, she got dressed in jeans and a sweater, as it was a sunless Sunday and the temperature had dropped twenty degrees overnight.

As she got into her car, she flipped on the radio to distract herself from thinking. Driving to the 405, she merged and was able to go the speed limit for a change. The pop song ended, and a commercial came on. She switched stations. "The California Lottery is now at $348 million. No one hit the six numbers. But there is a lucky person or persons who bought a ticket at a 7-Eleven in West L.A. who may have won almost two million dollars as they matched five out of six numbers. The numbers are: 6 23 29 32 42 and 44."

Yolanda exited at Wilshire Boulevard and turned down the first side street she saw so she could pull over and find her lottery ticket. She pulled her purse onto her lap and shakily reached in to find her wallet. It was one of those multiple pocketed and zippered things and she couldn't remember which compartment she'd placed it in. She checked the coin section and found some change. She looked at her checkbook, yanked it out, and turned it upside down. Nothing. In the money compartment, there were a few bills wedged inside, mostly singles. She counted sixteen dollars. *Crap, I gotta go to the ATM.*

As she put the money back, the ticket fluttered to the floor. Leaning down to pick it up, her head banged into the steering wheel, and she saw stars. Her nerves were jangled as she looked at the ticket upside down and then flipped it right side up. Now what the hell were the numbers?

The radio announcer was talking about the grand opening of a new family restaurant in Arcadia. She flipped through the dial, but nothing about the lottery numbers was heard. iPhone! She switched it on, got a signal, found the lottery website, and saw the numbers. Comparing the numbers on screen to those on her ticket, she read them three times before being convinced that she had indeed matched five of them! Five numbers meant what -- a million dollars? Two million dollars? What had the man said? She smiled and laughed and the pain in her forehead vanished. She pounded on the steering wheel. The realization of winning so much money and being able to save the shelter and finally open Yolanda's Yummery hit her with the most glorious dose of reality she'd ever experienced.

But it didn't get out of control. She looked around, knowing that being in possession of an un-turned in lottery ticket and yelling about it wasn't the best idea in the world. Making sure her car doors were locked, she glanced at her surroundings. It was going to be a long drive to her parents' home, but she knew she had to tell them in person. Driving quickly down the street, she giggled as she thought about how she'd tell her parents the incredible news.

***

The ecstatic Carter family sat in the breakfast nook with Carson curled up on his dad's lap. He sensed the joy in the air.

"Okay, now that you've signed the ticket you should take it to the lottery office." Abby was looking at her tablet. "There are a few locations, but they open at eight on Monday."

She sighed. "Wow, this will be a very long day and night for me!" She petted the cat. "I can be late for work, but I don't want to let anyone know I've won."

"I figured that was the case," her dad said. "So, we should talk to a lawyer about this. I think a blind trust would work in your case."

"I still can't believe I won!" Her voice was more animated than usual. "I'm rich!" she said. "I'm really rich, and now I can finally have my yummery!"

Chapter 11

Yolanda kept the knowledge that she had won $1,879,294.21 between herself and her family.

That secret lasted for a few weeks until the obvious signs of spending became clear.

Zac was smart enough to figure out that she'd come into some money when the Crown Street Cat Shelter was renovated with another room and the staff's earnings increased. The big tip-off was the lease of a large retail space in the brand-new Brentwood Grove Shoppes strip mall on San Vicente and Grove Street. Yolanda's Yummery found its home in a 3,500 square-foot end unit. The details she had to endure to make sure the yummery was up and running within a year were a crash course in business ownership.

Zac approached Yolanda one night in April, as she was unloading groceries from her car. "Hey Yolanda, wait!" He was spiffed up in a dress shirt and jeans, so he didn't look like he'd spent most of the day at Green Palms. Holding a large bouquet of red, pink, and yellow gladiolas and roses showed some thoughtfulness, so she let him inside as she thanked him for the flowers. She put them in a vase and admired the bountiful array of springtime blossoms.

"Look, Yo, I've been brainstorming with some investors about my own mini-golf course that will be in a biodome out in Simi Valley. It'll be awesome, like completely one of a kind! It'll be open 24/7 and it won't matter what the weather's like -- it'll always be perfect for mini golf inside."

"That's nice, Zac. Could you please put that jug of apple juice on the counter?"

"I'll call it Biodome Valley Mini Golf and I think it's the best idea ever. You know how much I love golf." He picked up the glass jug and put it on the counter. "And I think it's a win-win situation with the investors and it'll make lots of money and we'll be even richer."

"Uh-huh." Yolanda picked up another bag of groceries and began removing some cans and bottles and placing them on the island.

"I'll let you sell your brownies at the concession stand."

"You'll let me? Thanks, that's real nice of you."

"I know. I mean, we've been friends for a long time so the way I look at it the money is at least half mine."

She finished unloading some mangoes when the urge to throw them at him almost overwhelmed her. "Let's talk about this some other time."

He was soon gone from the premises, and she looked at the cats that had just ambled into the kitchen. "Gee whiz, kitties, what do you think of Biodome mini golf? And for me to sell my brownies at a *concession stand?*" She laughed and shook her head as they stared at her. "Yeah, right, imagine me investing in an updated version of putt-putt? I don't think so!"

***

Frederick Carter hoisted the dolly into the bed of the rented pickup truck. He waited as Yolanda hurried down the driveway carrying a couple of stainless steel shelves. "Yolanda, I said I'd get those."

"It's okay, dad." She placed them into the back of the truck. He reached in and straightened one of them.

She glanced back at the house with the twin palm trees on either side of the front door. A hunched-over man waved at her.

Yolanda and her dad waved back and got inside the beige pickup. Her dad started the engine and drove down the quiet residential street.

"Gus told me he was a baker for sixty-two years," she said.

Frederick nodded. "That's a mighty long time. And he almost gave away that baker's rack. I've learned a lot about baking equipment these past few months and that brand's very expensive – even used."

"Yeah, he didn't seem concerned about the money. He just said he wanted it to go to a nice new home," Yolanda remarked.

"It's great that he feels that way."

Yolanda smiled and then looked through the dusty windshield. "That's where you turn right."

"Okay. You sure you want to do this?"

"Yes, dad, I'm sure. Once you get to the first stop sign, hang a left on Woodland Canyon."

Her father smiled and followed the directions. "Okay, my navigator."

Yolanda was watching the scenery rolling past, noticing the houses growing larger and further back from the newly paved road. "Looks a little too nice for a dog shelter."

"Right you are, my young detective." He rolled down his window and looked out into the glare of the late afternoon sun. Even with the air conditioning on, the heat was causing him to sweat. "Way too nice."

Slamming on the brakes, the truck stopped in front of a gated entrance. *Rancho Camarillo* the sign said in gold letters.

It was an exclusive gated community. To the right of the gate was a prominent sign: Private community. Residents and guests only.

They looked at each other.

"Looks like a hoity toity place," said Frederick.

"This isn't anything like I thought it would be," she commented. "So, what are you waiting for? It's 13767."

"I guess I could say we're making a delivery…"

A shiny black Ferrari drove around them, and the driver stopped in front of the card slot and punched in a code. They watched as the gates slid open. The sports car sped inside, almost hitting the moving gate. Frederick gunned the engine and followed the car.

"Good job, Dad," Yolanda commented as they drove past a white brick mansion with a large fountain in the front yard. "What a waste of water in this drought."

He shook his head. "I know. Look at the numbers on your side because I don't see any over here. I hate it when people hide their addresses."

"Yeah, especially inside a gated community."

He drove slowly as she stared out the open window, observing the addresses. "Okay, I see 65 so it should be the next one. Now get your phone ready to take pictures."

Yolanda wiped off her phone's screen on her shirt. "It is. Like they say, pictures or it didn't happen." She aimed and clicked as soon as he stopped at the end of the street, just past the house.

They looked at the large contemporary home with tall windows. Some construction equipment was parked to one side and a port-a-potty was at the edge of the property near a couple of dumpsters.

"I think maybe the Other Patrick Stewart should look into this."

Her father turned the steering wheel and backed out. "You're right. Let's take more pictures and then we'll leave."

Yolanda and her father leaned out of the open windows and snapped a few shots with their camera phones. She giggled. "This is cool, Dad." She paused, looking around. "I don't see anyone. Let's go take a look."

"Yolanda, I don't think that's such a wise idea."

"It's cool, park over there and…"

Frederick glanced into the rear-view mirror. "Nope." He turned around, as did she. A black-and-white patrol car was speeding towards them. "Probably not your friendly neighborhood watch. Let's go."

She held onto the door handle while her father floored it, doing a 180, tires squealing. Her mouth hung open as she stared at her father and then glanced at the passenger's side mirror, noting the distance as the car seemed to get closer, but after screeching around a bend and turning down a side street, the other vehicle vanished.

Gripping the steering wheel, he yanked it to the left and the pickup went down a bumpy vacant lot and behind a gray two-story house. Nervously, he looked around at the neighborhood. "We should be okay here for now…"

"Wow, Dad, I've never seen you drive like that before."

"Yolanda, have I ever told you about the time I saw *Smokey and the Bandit?*"

Chapter 12

Yolanda emailed Rocky Montoya's address and photos to *The Other Patrick Stewart*. Unlike the Carters, he was able to get access to the home and surrounding property. His investigation uncovered a fraud that gained him a larger audience.

Blogdate: 09-04.
Topic: Wicked Fun Gentlemen's Club Dogs Live High Life!
By Patrick Stewart [click to watch full report]
Readers,
What do men and dogs have in common? Jacuzzis, mirrored ceilings, stripper poles, and infinity pools!

Yes, folks, the new Rocky Montoya Dog Rescue Mission will have it all for our four-legged friends.

Located in an exclusive gated community, the ten-bedroom, nine-(full)-bathroom contemporary home on five acres is owned by Mr. Rocky Montoya, owner of the Wicked Fun Gentlemen's Club. In February, (Mr. Montoya who is also a co-owner of Freeze N Bake), was a runner-up in the Great Brownie Taste-off, generously sponsored by Planet Coffee Café. Yolanda Carter of the Crown Street Cat Shelter created the event to stop the Freeze N Bake Corporation from buying out the non-profit cat shelter. While Ms. Carter was the winner of the Taste-off, the donations the shelter received were slightly less than Mr. Montoya's, which totaled $10,337.80. This amount was earmarked to help build the dog rescue mission. However, nowhere in Ventura County has a permit been filed to build a rescue mission. The area in question is zoned only for private residences and the HOA for the community has a ban on anyone owning more than two dogs per household.

A recent journey to the site of the dog shelter revealed a private residence inside the prestigious Rancho Camarillo gated community. Upon further investigation, we learned that the 11,450-square-foot home includes a gourmet kitchen, butler's pantry (handy for preparing all that dog food), a wet bar, wine cellar with tasting room, a Jacuzzi, koi pond, and infinity pool. In one of the bedrooms there's a stripper pole and mirrored ceilings and the others boast a stunning view of the Ojai Valley. Yes, we think there will be some happy dogs running around this "shelter," only they'll be the two-legged variety.

Upon learning we'd discovered his misuse of the donations, Montoya states that we are "barking up the wrong tree."

After Yolanda read the blog, she expelled a deep breath. It wasn't surprising – and yet it was. Lying about helping animals and appropriating the funds for oneself -- that was down and dirty. When she went to her parents' house that night, she gave them a copy of the article. They agreed with her sentiments.

Mostly the meeting revolved around the plans for the Yummery and the completion of the logo, which incorporated the three colors: lemon yellow, sea foam green and pastel pink. Working with her parents created a closer bond and their input into the bakery was based on their extensive business experience.

Abby designed the logo to fit on items that would sell in the yummery's store. Yolanda wanted to add chef's caps, jackets, and other apparel worn in bakeries, but Abby told her if she wanted to sell to the public, she couldn't have a huge selection. "Dear, the Gift Corner is only 100-square-feet. We won't have room for everything!" So, it was narrowed down to aprons, T-shirts and tank tops, tote bags, potholders, and baseball caps.

Frederick's glass creations would be used throughout the yummery so they could be seen, and only a few cake stands would be put on the Gift Corner's glass shelves. Ever since the elongated cat vase designs were featured in *Los Angeles* magazine, orders for his work had increased greatly.

Yolanda reflected on the vast amount of time and effort it took to wade through the mountain of paperwork involved in launching a new business in Los Angeles County, particularly the neighborhood of Brentwood.

***

Heather, the lotion-and-soap maker opened her manufacturing plant in a Culver City warehouse park. "No more kitchen stove for me," the woman told Yolanda as she drove to work for her first official day. The successful Nautical Nor'easter line shipped to over 250 locations nationwide. A small selection of her special bakery-themed lotions and soaps such as chocolate brownie, red velvet, and vanilla buttercream would be sold in the Gift Corner section of Yolanda's Yummery.

***

As the grand opening loomed ever closer, Yolanda grew increasingly anxious about what could be a cataclysmic failure. Most new businesses didn't succeed, and that fact kept circulating around her head every night. Was the alarm system for the store adequate? Would there be enough parking spaces for the customers? No, she wouldn't call them that; they would be called appreciated guests, because that's what they were. No matter if they walked in and bought a single cookie, or a dozen gift-wrapped brownies or the unique Magical Cakes of Love.

How many fifty-pound bags of flour and sugar would she need to order? What about getting a deal on bulk chocolate and all the other ingredients she'd need?

Zac sometimes stopped by the yummery when she was there. He did nothing but get underfoot. Usually someone else was there to shoo him away. Then he'd stop by her house and pester her about the Biodome Valley Mini Golf idea. He'd suggested they get married so they could be better business partners. She knew he wanted to get his hands on her lottery winnings.

Driving home late one night, she recalled how romantic the dream of having one's own bakery had seemed when she was younger. The notion of baking dozens of cupcakes and decorating them anyway she wanted seemed so wonderful. As did choosing her own menu, using the best ingredients, and coming up with creative names for her sweet treats. Now her visions of what owning a bakery entailed were somewhat different from her romantic-and-sugary daydreams.

Chapter 13

On the last Saturday in February, at eight o'clock in the morning, Yolanda's Yummery was finally open for business. The crowd that gathered included her family and friends, and many of the cat shelter workers and volunteers.

She wore a yellow Yolanda's Yummery T-shirt and jeans and a pale-pink logoed apron. Her hair was worn in an elegant French twist. Unable to sleep, she had arrived a little past midnight to bake all the goodies, most of them to be given away. As for counter help, she hired four part-timers including Jeannie Stanton, a retired secretary who wanted to work at a bakery part time, because she "loved the environment."

Jeannie walked into Yolanda's Yummery on her first day of work, absorbing the new surroundings with a look of awe. To her left was the Gift Corner. She noticed a spiral clothes rack featuring colorful aprons, T-shirts, and tank tops bearing the cute logo.

They were standing in front of the curved glass display case that housed the personal-sized cakes and the signature brownies. Atop each case sat three glass trays with domed lids.

Jeannie looked at Yolanda with a puzzled expression. "I've never heard of Magical Cakes of Love, but I love the name."

Laughing, Yolanda pointed to the case displaying the single and double-layer cakes. "They're smaller than layer cakes. But I think calling them Magical Cakes of Love makes them sound way more romantic. And, so far, all my testers have loved them!" She lifted the lid and picked out a sample. "Please try a slice."

"Certainly!" Jeannie took a cupcake liner filled with a rich red rectangle featuring two layers of white frosting. After the first dainty bite, she smiled.

Abby hurried up to Jeannie and gave her a hug. "I'm so happy you're here today, Jeannie! That's such a nice headband."

"Thank you so much. My daughter made it for me," Jeannie said.

"Yolanda's highly creative—in the kitchen. For me it's about fiber art." Abby pointed to her brightly colored batik-print T-shirt in neon pink, yellow, and green. "I love the art of batik, and it took me a while to learn how to do it to my satisfaction. But once I learned there was no stopping me."

Abby noticed twin boys dressed in matching jeans and navy-blue polo shirts. "Yoo-hoo, boys, would you like a balloon?" She stepped over to a beribboned bundle tied to the back of one of the chairs and removed a pair of them in yellow.

"Your mother's so nice," Jeannie said.

"Yeah, most of the time." Yolanda chuckled and pointed to the case that ran opposite the door and extended almost to the back of the store. "Now this is where we'll be stocking all our cookies and cupcakes. We also want to offer samples throughout the day; it'll be easy to just cut a cookie in quarters, and we're doing mini cupcakes but that won't be offered regularly except by the dozen."

Jeannie looked at the colorful array of cookies, many of them wearing brilliant sanding sugar coats. "They're so beautiful," she said.

"Thank you. I managed to get them done just before the store officially opened. You know that starting on Monday we'll officially open at seven. Oh, by the way, make sure you give a free brownie to every customer who buys a Magical Cake of Love."

Her father added a tray of chocolate cupcakes topped with multicolored sprinkles to the display case. "Jeannie, this is my father, Frederick," Yolanda said.

He grinned and stepped around the case to shake Jeannie's hand.

"Oh my, are you the one who made all these gorgeous cake stands?"

Frederick reached for her hand and shook it. "Guilty as charged. So glad to have you aboard, Jeannie."

She beamed. "Thank you, so glad to be here! I read about you in *Los Angeles* magazine. I love your work."

He chuckled. "Most kind of you. But I'm just a simple glassblower, ma'am. We have lots of hot air in our lungs, that's all. My daughter's the one with all the talent. I swear I can't eat another cupcake right now, yet I'm not stuffed too full. And let me tell you it's better than the first jolt of caffeine you get from a good cuppa joe. I think there's something magical about all her baked goods. Then again, I guess it's just the proud papa in me." He gave his daughter a warm embrace.

"Thanks, Dad. By the way, I need to do something about the coffee and tea…"

"A cue for me to check the beverage invoices in the office and get it stocked." He gave a wave and trotted back to the kitchen area behind the cookies and cupcakes counter.

Yolanda led the way to a small, glass-fronted, stainless steel refrigerator unit that was at the back wall. It was loaded with small bottles of milk, iced tea, flavored and sparkling water, and soft drinks. "Here are the cold drinks; we also have free coffee, tea, and hot chocolate today."

She turned around and pointed to the eight round, white tables, each with four matching chairs around them. They lined the wall from back to front on the other side of the cookies and cupcakes display case. The pastel-striped cushions were the same color as the wallpaper.

"Authentic vintage ice cream parlor tables and chairs from the sixties. The things I found online," Yolanda exclaimed.

"Those really make the bakery so warm and inviting," Jeannie noted.

A young couple sat down, the mother holding an infant dressed in pastel-blue knitwear. They put down their paper cups of coffee and both had mini cupcake samples and each a full-size brownie. The mother bit into the brownie and closed her eyes as she slowly chewed. Her husband inhaled the chocolate cupcake.

Yolanda greeted the pair and learned they'd read about the Great Brownie Taste-off review and resulting press about the fake dog shelter on The Other Patrick Stewart's blog. Neither of them could wait to try the winning brownies once they learned that Yolanda's Yummery was opening on the west side of town. "We love these brownies so much we're going to buy a dozen and tell all our friends about this fantastic yummery," said the mother.

By now, the crowds surging in kept the counter help occupied. The high-tech computerized point of sale system was versatile yet simple to use. The other two employees Yolanda had hired last week were local college students, Trina Allman and Nick Delaney.

Heather and Barry Hathaway made a brief appearance. Barry was tall and large boned, and his untucked black polo shirt didn't hide his expanding waistline. He was enjoying the samples and after stuffing a mini brownie into his mouth, he hugged his slender wife. "Baby, I love you more than I've ever loved anyone." She returned the hug with equal fervor and Yolanda thought that maybe she'd have to get the fire extinguisher out of the kitchen before Heather gently pulled away.

"You're the best husband a woman could ever have." She gave him a quick kiss, noticing a few people looking at them. "Now let's see how the lotions and cupcake soaps are doing."

The bearish man nodded, stroked her cheek once, and followed his wife over to the Gift Corner.

Patrick Stewart sauntered in and made a beeline for the Magical Cakes of Love sample tray. "Hey, Yolanda, what time can you do the interview?"

Yolanda looked at the cupcake-shaped wall clock above the front door. "How about in five minutes?"

Grabbing two vanilla buttercream slices, he handed one to Louie, his cameraman. "Sounds doable." He quickly scarfed down his piece and smiled. "Outstanding cake, Yolanda," he said, then winked at her. "I wonder why you call them Magical Cakes of Love!"

Just then, Teagan Mishkin strutted into the bakery, wearing a snug French-cut T-shirt and a pair of tight jeans. Her now-darker blonde hair was pulled into a high ponytail, and instead of stilettos, she wore white-leather sneakers. Both Patrick and Louie stared at the new arrival. "Haven't I seen you at another event...wait, you were at the Great Brownie Taste-off!"

"Maybe I was." Teagan slowly sashayed to the back of the store. Three UCLA-sweatshirt-wearing young men studied her feminine walk and promptly sampled a couple of mini cupcakes apiece. Even as she pushed aside the pink-and-yellow striped curtain that concealed the kitchen, and was gone from view, they almost dislocated their necks trying to catch a glimpse.

Louie sampled a brownie and when he thought no one was looking, snatched a second piece. He switched on his camera before Patrick had a chance to pick up his mic, but it was evident that he was filming the bakery. The camera was zooming around the room and focusing on the display cases, the samples, and the many appreciated guests. The tables were all filled, and a few people had brought along their cell phones, tablets and laptops to take advantage of the free Wi-Fi.

Yolanda and Teagan were back in the kitchen, conversing about Teagan's upcoming shift. She put on a yellow apron and tied the strings tightly around her small waist. "I'm working here part time 'cause I understand lots of producers and directors live around here."

Yolanda handed her a small paper menu. "You saw this in the email I sent you."

Teagan glanced at it. "Yeah." She giggled. "It looks a lot better than the lap dance list and song-count chart we had at the Wicked Fun Gentlemen's Club. Ooh, I love chocolate cupcakes."

"I'm glad. I know that Rocky's business is down after the hoopla surrounding the fake dog shelter."

"Tell me about it. No more $900 nights. I'm lucky to get maybe $400 or $500 on weekends, so unless it gets even worse, I can only work here 'til five on Saturday. It really sucks, but the club still pays better than most places. What he did was so wrong. I thought he liked dogs, but he doesn't even care about them. He just stole those dog pictures off the internet."

"No, I don't see how he could and then pull a stunt like that. I'm glad to hear that he was forced to sell the Ojai house." Yolanda glanced at her watch. "Okay, I've got an interview. You just sell, sell, sell the sweets, Teagan."

She burst out laughing. "I'm really good at it."

"That's why I think you're going to do really well, and I think the tips jar will be full whenever you work." She gave her friend a quick hug and rushed out into the bakery to give her very first interview in Yolanda's Yummery.

After Yolanda had wrapped up the interview. She'd allowed her employees to be interviewed. Missy and Roger stopped by. The couple was delighted with the samples and made several purchases, and had extra freebies thrown in, including a chocolate Magical Cake of Love.

Wanda from Sweet Spot Baking Supplies stopped by to congratulate her. "I'm so proud of you, this yummery is awesome. One of a kind!"

"Just like your store," Yolanda told the young woman, handing her a walnut brownie. "You'll recognize that special French chocolate!"

A bearded man wearing a white-and-navy yacht cap marched inside. "Free samples! Oh, goody!" The chubby man wore an open navy captain's jacket revealing a soiled white undershirt. His baggy trousers were held in place by suspenders. The captain looked around the busy bakery and spotted Teagan holding a tray of cookie samples. He scratched his gray beard and reached for a chocolate chip cookie. "You got a nice rack, dearie." He greedily grabbed two cookie halves and shoved them into his mouth. Chewing quickly, his smile widened, and crumbs fell to his belly and the floor. "Mmmm. Great cookies," he declared.

"Glad you like them, sir," Teagan said, turning away to offer cookies to some of the appreciated guests waiting in line to buy sweets.

He aggressively followed her, reaching for the tray and snatched another handful. He barely glanced at the nutty, oatmeal raisin cookies as he crammed them into his mouth. "Um, um," he grunted, merely chewing and moaning in delight. After he swallowed the last morsel he said, "Will you marry me, missy? I got a yacht at the marina, and we can have a shipboard wedding."

Teagan grinned. "No thanks, I'm engaged."

Yolanda's father was wending his way over from the far side of the store. He held a yellow cellophane bag containing six cookies. It was tied with a matching ribbon and sported a colorful hangtag. "Here you go, sir, it's on the house." Frederick handed the cookies to the captain.

"Why thank you, good sir. Ahoy mate to you." He saluted Frederick and stuffed the cookies inside his undershirt as he glanced longingly at Teagan. "You sure we can't get married?"

Teagan grinned and shook her head just as an old woman in a hot pink tracksuit wielding a cane hobbled over and grabbed a cookie sample. "I'm single, Mr. Captain!"

"Unsurprising," the captain stated as he thrust out his chest and strode towards the front door.

The bustling bakery remained like that all day. Even though it was overcast, it didn't rain, so that also helped business. A few minutes before closing, according to the cupcake clock, a handsome man in a tan, glen-plaid suit and polished, black loafers strolled in. His wavy brown hair with golden highlights emphasized his classical features, and his piercing dark eyes caught Yolanda's attention at once. The man looked around the yummery. Few items remained in the cases. The trays containing samples were nearly empty.

"This yummery looks quite posh," he said to Yolanda who was standing near the door. "But then again, I've never been to a yummery before...even in Los Angeles."

For an instant, she was flummoxed, as he was the sensuous and smoldering man she'd seen in her vision of the beach. She hid her shock and switched over to her sensible business personality.

"I call it a yummery because everything I bake here is yummy. I've created my own brand."

"You're quite confident, aren't you?"

"Yes I am. Would you like to sample a brownie?" She reached for the tray and extended it to him. "I'm sorry that we have so few samples left…"

"Please, don't be. Obviously, people are finding your products to be quite…yummy!" The handsome man with the English accent reached for a brownie chunk and tossed it into his mouth. There was a pause as his smirk turned into a close-mouthed smile, and his eyes brightened. "Indeed, I think this is yummy. Let me buy the rest of your stock."

There were only two brownies left. She smiled and went around the counter to put them in a bag. "No, since you're the last customer of the day I'll give you a 100% discount."

"That's more than kind of you." He watched her intently. It was as though he knew her, yet he'd never even seen her until he walked into the uniquely named yummery.

Only the glass counter separated them as she was immersed in the attention of the highly appreciated guest. The annoying noise of a loud car horn followed by screeching brakes caused her to look up. She rolled her eyes when she saw where the noise was coming from.

A black BMW roared into a nearby parking space. The driver rushed out of the car and slammed the door shut with his hip. In his arms he held a big, white teddy bear. "Yolanda!"

The man turned and watched as Zac rushed towards them and opened the door, dashing over to the counter. The teddy bear had a grin on its plush face and a big, red heart on its chest. Zac's breathing was ragged, as he noticed the well-dressed gentleman leaning on the counter and Yolanda not leaning away.

He thumped the teddy bear down on the counter and stood next to the stranger.

She looked at her former boyfriend and the teddy bear as if seeing an alien emerging from a UFO. Was that a belated Valentine's Day gift? Unsure of whether to laugh, Zac's intense gaze suggested that might be misinterpreted.

Outside, a cacophony of horns caused her to look up in the direction of the parking lot. The appreciated guest turned and ran toward the door.

"Zac!" Yolanda yelled, pointing at the window.

His car was rolling backwards, and an SUV was in its path.

The Englishman was outside along with another man who was attempting to stop the rolling BMW.

Zac turned around and saw his car about to crash and two men trying to stop it.

"No! Don't get your dirty fingerprints on my car. I just waxed it."

The car was pushed back to safety and Zac was busy with his microfiber cloth wiping away the smudge marks.

The Englishman returned to the counter and was grinning at Yolanda.

"That man's a bit of a wanker, isn't he?"

A loud laugh was heard from behind the curtain. "You got that right, friend," said Yolanda's father, as he walked over to the door. "Almost time to close up for your first day, daughter."

She glanced up at the clock. "Thanks, we still have five more minutes."

The well-dressed man was holding his bag of brownies. "My name's Nigel Garvey. I'd like to learn more about your yummery...and about you."

The End

The Winning Brownie Recipe

After more than a dozen attempts, I finally achieved a much better winning brownie recipe. While I've always liked brownies, I've never loved them. This recipe is one I love and am happy to share it with you. I used the European baking chocolate and powdered cocoa, along with high quality butter, and a healthy sugar alternative: organic coconut palm sugar. The blend makes for a super-rich, fudgy brownie. I recommend using Valrhona chocolate *feves* or the Callebaut callets if you have them on hand or can get them easily enough. If not, use any type of high quality 70% cacao content chocolate.

Your butter should be good quality and unsalted is recommended. You will taste the butter in this brownie recipe due to the amount used.

If possible, use pasture-range eggs, as they taste better.

I used an 8" x 8" glass baking dish. You can use a 9" x 9" glass or metal baking dish if you prefer, but the brownies will be slightly flatter.

If you don't have a double boiler, substitute a pot with a heat-proof glass bowl over it. Make sure to add a small amount of water so the bowl doesn't get wet.

INGREDIENTS:

- 1/2 cup [1 stick] unsalted butter, melted

- 1 cup organic coconut palm sugar

- 2 eggs [room temperature]

- 1/2 cup [4 ounces] dark chocolate

- 2 teaspoons pure vanilla extract or vanilla bean paste

- 1/2 cup all-purpose flour, sifted

- 2 Tablespoons cocoa powder, Dutch processed, sifted

INSTRUCTIONS:

- Preheat oven to 325 degrees.

- Grease your pan with butter.

- Sift the cocoa powder and flour together in a small bowl. Set aside.

- Chop up chocolate if using a bar. Melt chocolate and butter together over a double boiler. Use low heat to ensure the chocolate doesn't seize.

- In a large bowl, add the sugar.

- Add an egg, mix well, then add the second egg and mix well.

- Stir in melted butter and chocolate mixture.

- Gently fold in flour and cocoa powder, until combined. Add the vanilla extract.

- Pour mixture into pan and bake for 30-35 minutes. Let the brownies cool completely. Cut into squares. Enjoy.

Want more brownie recipes? Check out:

Baking Chocolate Cupcakes and Brownies: A Beginner's Guide

It's easier than ever to bake decadent chocolate cupcakes and brownies. Get helpful tips about decorating and coloring cupcakes, recommended equipment, and loads of resources. Original and tested step-by-step recipes include Blueberry Brownies, Chocolate Coconut Cupcakes, Blue Velvet Cupcakes, Peppermint Swirl Cupcakes, and many more tantalizing treats.

The book was written by someone who went from baking box mix brownies and cupcakes to discovering the joy of baking from scratch. With a photograph of each finished treat, the reader will be inspired to try baking these delicious recipes.

About The Author

Lisa Maliga is an American author of contemporary fiction and cozy mysteries. Her nonfiction titles consist of how to make bath and body products with an emphasis on melt and pour soap crafting. When researching her fourth cozy mystery, she discovered the art of baking French macarons. She has written three dessert cookbooks, including two on macarons. When not writing, Lisa reads an assortment of books, takes photos, skates, and is working on a series of baking and soaping books and video tutorials.

You'll find more about her work at:

http://www.lisamaliga.com

http://lisamaliga.wordpress.com/

https://truthsocial.com/@lisamaliga

http://pinterest.com/lisamaliga/

https://www.youtube.com/user/LisaMaligaCreates

Newsletter - http://eepurl.com/UZbE9

Author's Note

Thank you for taking the time to read *The Great Brownie Taste-off (A Yolanda's Yummery Cozy Mystery, Book 1)*. Feel free to write a review on any of the online bookstores. Also, please tell your friends, family, and friendly librarian about this book, along with any of my other titles!

Other Titles by the Author

FICTION:

Diary of a Hollywood Nobody - Chris Yarborough is a Midwesterner as green as the corn back home in Ohio. This former bookstore employee moves out to Los Angeles to pursue a profitable career in screenwriting.

Hollywood After Dark: 3 Tales of Terror – [Paperback and eBook] This trio of horror novelettes takes place in Los Angeles and Hollywood. Titles include: Satan's Casting Call, An Author's Nightmare, and Hollywood Starz Storage.

I Almost Married a Narcissist - Charlotte White falls in love with a younger Romanian gymnastics coach. Andrei Antonescu is a sexy and handsome foreigner who loves to have fun and flirt with the ladies. The more she gets to know him, the more red flags are unfurled. Once she's able to see past his good looks and muscular body, Charlotte is unprepared for some shocking revelations.

I WANT YOU: Seduction Emails from a Narcissist - Arlen J. Stevenson is a narcissist who uses his scant literary accomplishments to entice his online victims. Meeting and seducing vulnerable women is what drives this Alabama-born man. [Paperback and eBook]

Love Me, Need Me: A Narcissist's Tale is about a bumbling sexual predator, narcissist, and author of three insipid zombie books. Middle-aged Arlen J. Stevenson hails from Alabama. His relentless and often hilarious pursuit of women online leads him to our other protagonist, Los Angeles-based writer of term papers, Helena Hoffman. [Paperback and eBook]

The Narcissist Chronicles: The WHOLE Story - Combined are the two narcissist novels: LOVE ME, NEED ME: A NARCISSIST'S TALE and I WANT YOU: SEDUCTION E-MAILS FROM A NARCISSIST.

North of Sunset - It's 1996 and Hollywood is thriving in the era of indulgences. Sherman Lee is a volatile and successful action movie producer who seeks critical acceptance. Ever the partier, his excesses are starting to take their toll. He can't keep a personal assistant more than a few days until Emily Karelin is sent to fill the position. She's a temp with no showbiz background, one of the requirements Sherman demands. [Paperback and eBook]

Out of the Blue - Sylvia Gardner is a naïve cashier who lives with her mother in Richport, Illinois. Upset with being dumped by her first boyfriend; she later falls in love with an English actor after watching him on a TV show. For two years, she researches Alexander Thorpe's life and career, saving her money to travel to his Cotswolds village, intent on meeting him. [Paperback and eBook]

Satan's Casting Call - Duncan Smith-Holmes is a struggling young actor who is in desperate need of a paying gig or he has to leave Hollywood.

September Harvest - In this slice-of-life story set in September 1979, we meet Laurie Caswell, a bookstore clerk at the Northbrook Mall. That Saturday night she goes to the movies with her boyfriend. Later, they go to her house and share some booze. After he leaves, she has a vivid dream of the dying mall in 2021 and is shocked at the darkness that engulfs the future. Is it a dream, a nightmare, a vision, or a prophecy?

South of Sunset - Such a world-renowned name conjures up images of movies, sunglass-wearing stars, palm trees, plastic surgery, drug habits, the proverbial overnight success ... and the happy ending. In this collection of original short fiction, the author takes us into the minds of an assortment of losers, dreamers, successes, wannabes, and has-beens.

Sweet Dreams - Brenda Nevins is a successful romance author with a movie deal, a reality TV show, and a forthcoming bakery. Complications arise whenever any communication she sends or receives turns into fragments of a science fiction story. Will she find whoever is responsible for hijacking her career, finances, and even her fiancé?

NONFICTION:

12 Easy Melt and Pour Soap Recipes - Contains original recipes, 37 color photos, and several places to buy soap base, molds, fragrances and other necessary supplies. Learn how easy it is to craft your own melt and pour soap in less than one hour!

Baking French Macarons: A Beginner's Guide - Bake beautiful and delicious French macarons in your own kitchen. This collection of tried-and-tested recipes allows bakers to create these tasty and colorful confections.

Baking Chocolate Cupcakes and Brownies: A Beginner's Guide - It's easier than ever to bake decadent chocolate cupcakes and brownies. Get helpful tips about decorating and coloring cupcakes, recommended equipment, and loads of resources.

Baking Macarons: The Swiss Meringue Method - With a photo of each recipe, this book offers everything you need to bake beautiful and delicious macarons. It features 20+ new tried-and-tested macaron recipes.

Dessert Cookbook Series: A Beginner's Guide - Includes 3 full-length dessert cookbooks and more than 55 recipes. Learn how to make many different desserts, no matter what your level of baking experience.

Fun Foodie Soap Crafting - You'll receive more than a dozen original and tested recipes, pretty packaging and labeling tips, 40+ photos, mistakes to avoid, and numerous supplier resources.

Happy Birthday Melt and Pour Soap Recipes - Say *Happy Birthday* with hand crafted soap! This unique book contains eight recipes for all budgets, melt and pour information, and birthday soap presentation tips. Contains 30+ color photos.

How to Make Handmade Shampoo Bars - Learn how easy it is to make natural handmade shampoo bars. This e-book contains 25+ recipes for shampoo bars, hair rinses, and hair masques. There are more than 50 color photos, step-by-step instructions, packaging tips and more. eBook format only.

How to Make Handmade Shampoo Bars: The Budget Edition - This innovative paperback includes 25+ recipes for shampoo bars, hair rinses, and hair masques. It contains many black and white photos, step-by-step instructions, and a chapter on natural additives. *Paperback format only.*

The Joy of Melt and Pour Soap Crafting - This eBook is written by someone who learned how to work with crafting glycerin melt & pour soap the hard way -- with only a single page of instructions to follow! If you've always wanted to make your own soap, here's an opportunity to learn just how easy it really is! Contains 40 recipes and MUCH more!

Kitchen Soap for Chefs: 4 Easy Melt & Pour Soap Recipes - It's easy to create chef's soap in your kitchen. Quickly cook up a batch of soap that will wash away strong kitchen odors. Now you can make excellent smelling and deodorizing soaps with four classic and carefully tested recipes.

Liquid African Black Soap Recipes for Skin and Hair - Make your own liquid African black soap in minutes! Includes five easy recipes using natural ingredients. You also receive information about essential oils and where to buy links for African black soap and other healthy additives.

Maple Sugar Melt & Pour Soap Recipe - Learn how to make a fun fall melt and pour soap recipe starring pure maple syrup—a healthy addition!

Matcha Green Tea Melt & Pour Soap Recipe - Learn how easy it is to make this luxurious melt and pour soap starring Matcha Green Tea. This type of soap is wonderful for all skin types and would make a great addition to any bath & body gift basket!

Monoi de Tahiti: Spa in a Bottle - What is Monoi de Tahiti and how will it benefit you? A bottle of this Polynesian beauty product has a variety of uses and will soothe your skin, hair, and nails. "Monoi de Tahiti: Spa in a Bottle" is a unique e-book focused on this fragrant and natural Tahitian beauty oil.

MORE Joy of Melt and Pour Soap Crafting - Two eBooks in one! You get "The Joy of Melt and Pour Soap Crafting" and "12 Easy Melt and Pour Soap Recipes" in one volume!

Nature's Beauty Oils: Monoi de Tahiti and Shea Butter - Two eBooks in one! Learn about nature's most versatile beauty oil and butter.

Nilotica [East African] Shea Body Butter Recipes [The Whipped Shea Butter Series], Book 1 - Learn the quickest and easiest way to whip Nilotica shea butter. Each recipe is easy to follow and includes the time it takes and amount it yields. Find out the secret to getting that incredibly light and airy texture.

Nuts About Shea Butter - The reader will discover shea butter's benefits, its numerous applications, and how to get optimal use from this healthy and natural nut fat. Learn about the differences between East African and West African shea butter.

Organic and Sulfate Free Melt and Pour Glycerin Soap Crafting Recipes - If you want to make the most natural soap without using lye, here is a way to craft organic and sulfate free melt and pour glycerin soap at home. In less than an hour, you can craft lovely organic, sulfate free and eco-friendly Castile soaps with these carefully tested recipes.

The Prepper's Guide to Soap Crafting and Soap Storage - Be the cleanest prepper around! Create your own lye-free soap or find the best type of soap to store in the coming years. Informative book shows the best ways to craft your own soap. You'll receive original recipes and valuable storage tips to get the most out of your soap. Learn about natural melt and pour, hand-milled, African black soap and liquid soaps. Includes recommended reading and several supplier resources.

Rooibos Tea and Pink Kaolin Shampoo Bar Recipe - Discover how to craft rebatch/hand-milled soap base into a unique and versatile shampoo bar for most hair types. Also includes a recipe for Rooibos tea and apple cider vinegar hair rinse.

The Soapmaker's Guide to Online Marketing - Soapmakers and crafters, learn how to grow your online presence! The Soapmaker's Guide to Online Marketing is packed with detailed information on designing, building, and promoting your website. Learn how to write a press release. Get loads of free promotional ideas. Attract customers by blogging, making videos, and showing off enticing photos of your soaps and/or other bath and body products.

Squirrels in the Hood - When Sunshine the cat departs in 2006, the second story balcony she occupied is very empty. Now that birds can be fed, the author does so, also attracting an array of hungry squirrels.

Vanilla Bean Melt & Pour Soap Recipe - Learn how easy it is to make this creamy melt and pour soap with natural vanilla beans. This type of soap is wonderful for all skin types and would make an excellent addition to any bath & body gift basket! Includes step-by-step photos!